ABORTION
Understanding the Controversy

By JoAnn Bren Guernsey

LERNER PUBLICATIONS COMPANY

MINNEAPOLIS

Front cover photographs are by Frances M. Roberts *(left)* and Richard B. Levine *(right)*.

Copyright © 1993 Lerner Publications Company

Library of Congress Cataloging-in-Publication Data

Guernsey, JoAnn Bren.
   Abortion : understanding the controversy / JoAnn Bren Guernsey.
     p. cm – (Pro/Con)
   Includes bibliographical references and index.
   Summary: Presents opposing viewpoints on abortion, discussing its biological, medical, and legal aspects.
   ISBN 0-8225-2605-0
1. Abortion–United States–Juvenile literature.
2. Pro-life movement–United States–Juvenile literature. 3. Pro-choice movement–United States–Juvenile literature. [1. Abortion.] I. Title. II. Series.
HQ767.5.U5G84   1992
363.4'6–dc20
                             91-42210
                                 CIP
                                 AC

Manufactured in the United States of America

1 2 3 4 5 6 98 97 96 95 94 93

CONTENTS

FOREWORD   4

1. DIFFICULT CHOICES   7

2. WHEN DOES LIFE BEGIN?   19

3. WOMANHOOD AND MOTHERHOOD   33

4. CRUSADERS FOR "LIFE" AND FOR "CHOICE"   39

5. THE MORALITY OF ABORTION   53

6. *ROE V. WADE*   61

7. LEGAL BATTLEGROUND   67

8. METHODS OF ABORTION   81

9. ALTERNATIVES TO ABORTION   91

SEEKING A COMMON GROUND   100

RESOURCES TO CONTACT   101

ENDNOTES   102

GLOSSARY   106

BIBLIOGRAPHY   108

INDEX   110

FOREWORD

If a nation expects to be ignorant and free,... it expects what never was and never will be.
                                                –Thomas Jefferson

Are you ready to participate in forming the policies of our government? Many issues are very confusing, and it can be difficult to know what to think about them or how to make a decision about them. Sometimes you must gather information about a subject before you can be informed enough to make a decision. Bernard Baruch, a prosperous American financier and an advisor to every president from Woodrow Wilson to Dwight D. Eisenhower, said, "If you can get all the facts, your judgment can be right; if you don't get all the facts, it can't be right."

But gathering information is only one part of the decision-making process. The way you interpret information is influenced by the values you have been taught since infancy–ideas about right and wrong, good and bad. Many of your values are shaped, or at least influenced, by how and where you grow up, by your race, sex, and religion, by how much money your family has. What your parents believe, what they read, and what you read and believe influence your decisions. The values of friends and teachers also affect what you think.

It's always good to listen to the opinions of people around you, but you will often confront contradictory points of view and points of view that are based not on fact, but on myth. John F. Kennedy, the 35th president of the United States, said, "The great enemy of the truth is very often not the lie–deliberate, contrived, and dishonest–

4

but the myth–persistent, persuasive, and unrealistic." Eventually you will have to separate fact from myth and make up your own mind, make your own decisions. Because you are responsible for your decisions, it's important to get as much information as you can. Then your decisions will be the right ones for you.

Making a fair and informed decision can be an exciting process, a chance to examine new ideas and different points of view. You live in a world that changes quickly and sometimes dramatically–a world that offers the opportunity to explore the ever-changing ground between yourself and others. Instead of forming a single, easy, or popular point of view, you might develop a rich and complex vision that offers new alternatives. Explore the many dimensions of an idea. Find kinship among an extensive range of opinions. Only after you've done this should you try to form your own opinions.

After you have formed an opinion about a particular subject, you may believe it is the only right decision. But some people will disagree with you and challenge your beliefs. They are not trying to antagonize you or put you down. They probably believe that they're right as sincerely as you believe you are. Thomas Macaulay, an English historian and author, wrote, "Men are never so likely to settle a question rightly as when they discuss it freely." In a democracy, the free exchange of ideas is not only encouraged, it's vital. Examining and discussing public issues and understanding opposing ideas are desirable and necessary elements of a free nation's ability to govern itself.

This Pro/Con series is designed to explore and examine different points of view on contemporary issues and to help you develop an understanding and appreciation of them. Most importantly, it will help you form your own opinions and make your own honest, informed decisions.

Mary Winget
Series Editor

DIFFICULT CHOICES

Perhaps no contemporary issue inspires more heated debate than abortion—the deliberate termination of a pregnancy. Some of you may have witnessed the bitterness in such a debate, and perhaps you have even felt this bitterness yourselves. Two best friends can sound like the worst enemies when engaged in an argument about abortion if one is strongly pro-choice (believes in the right to choose a safe, legal abortion) and the other is just as strongly pro-life (believes that abortion is murder, and therefore wrong).

Why is the debate over abortion so emotional? One reason is simply that people with opposing viewpoints on this issue share little common language. For example, many anti-abortionists refer to an unborn child (at whatever stage of development it happens to be) as a baby, while a pro-choice advocate calls it a **fetus.** Even such fundamental words as *life* and *murder* may have drastically different meanings for people on opposing sides of this issue.

The debate is bitter for another reason: each side tends to ignore or discount the arguments of the other. The fundamental question is, "Should abortion be legal?" The

7

debate, however, usually strays from this basic issue. For example, pro-choice advocates try to convince their opponents that women's rights are at stake. Pro-life supporters argue that the rights of the fetus are as important as those of the mother, and that abortion is murder. Other pro-choice defenders argue that if abortion *is* murder, why do so many pro-life advocates fight against the most logical methods of preventing this so-called genocide—birth control and sex education?[1]

A third reason for the bitterness of this debate is that most pro-choice and pro-life advocates reached their conclusions about abortion very early in life, probably even earlier than they can remember. They were taught by previous generations that there was only one correct point of view. Many people have trouble seeing why others who were brought up with the opposite viewpoint cannot simply look at the "facts" and be persuaded to change their minds. Dialogue becomes even more difficult when one side dismisses the other as "ignorant" or "bigoted."[2]

Tempers flare when opponents resort to oversimplification, because the issue is not simple. According to recent public opinion polls, the majority of Americans (at least 60 percent) hold beliefs that place them somewhere between the two most extreme, or radical, positions on the abortion issue.[3] Although radical groups on both sides of the issue may get the most media attention, most Americans have moderate viewpoints. Individuals in this moderate middle may lean toward pro-choice or pro-life, but they seek a middle ground.

Most people feel uncomfortable with abortion and are troubled by many of the reasons given for having one; but these same people are also uncomfortable with the government's interference in a woman's right to choose an abortion, a right granted in 1973 by the landmark Supreme Court decision in *Roe v. Wade.*

Half the adults surveyed by the *New York Times* in 1989 supported the availability of safe, legal abortions while only 9 percent felt that no abortions at all should be permitted.[4] Similarly, when Gallup pollsters asked a general question about the right of a woman to *choose* an abortion, a majority favored such a right. But when asked more specific questions, a majority also noted a need to distinguish among abortion choices and supported measures to restrict the procedure.[5]

Other polls show that many Americans are poorly informed about the abortion issue, and that they drastically underestimate the number of abortions performed each year—approximately 1.6 million, almost one-fourth of all pregnancies.[6] In addition, most Americans assume that many abortions are performed in cases of rape or incest, or in order to save the life of the mother. In reality, only about 1 percent of the 1.6 million abortions are performed for those reasons.[7]

If this is so, who are the women having abortions in the United States, and why are they having them? In one estimate, if current trends continue, approximately 46 percent —almost half—of all American women will have had at least one abortion by the time they are 45 years old.[8] Two national surveys were conducted in 1987 and 1988. Of the survey sample of nearly 12,000 women who obtained abortions in over 100 facilities, "almost 3 out of every 100 women aged 15-44 has [*sic*] an abortion each year."[9] The typical American woman who makes this choice is unmarried and under 30—probably 18 or 19 years old. Over 400,000 abortions, or one-fourth of the total number, are performed on teenagers

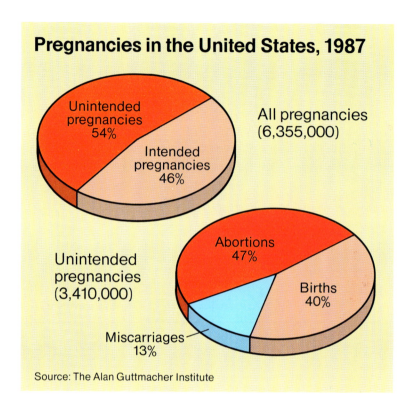

Pregnancies in the United States, 1987

Unintended pregnancies 54%

Intended pregnancies 46%

All pregnancies (6,355,000)

Abortions 47%

Births 40%

Unintended pregnancies (3,410,000)

Miscarriages 13%

Source: The Alan Guttmacher Institute

each year. Poor women are 30 times more likely to have abortions than those who are not poor. And women of color are more likely than white women to choose abortion.[10]

The reasons given for having an abortion usually include the belief that having a baby would interfere with work, school, or other responsibilities. Most women who choose abortion say they cannot afford to have a child, they do not want to be a single parent, or they have problems with the relationship they are in. About half the women having abortions became pregnant in spite of using some form of birth control. And 7 out of every 10 women who choose abortion say they intend to have children in the future.[11]

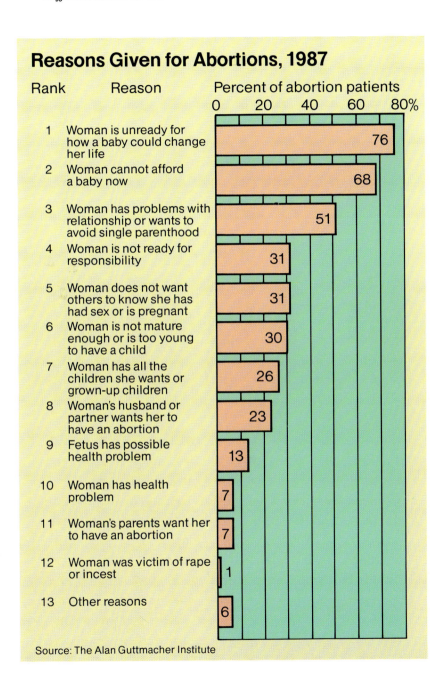

Reasons Given for Abortions, 1987

Rank	Reason	Percent of abortion patients
1	Woman is unready for how a baby could change her life	76
2	Woman cannot afford a baby now	68
3	Woman has problems with relationship or wants to avoid single parenthood	51
4	Woman is not ready for responsibility	31
5	Woman does not want others to know she has had sex or is pregnant	31
6	Woman is not mature enough or is too young to have a child	30
7	Woman has all the children she wants or grown-up children	26
8	Woman's husband or partner wants her to have an abortion	23
9	Fetus has possible health problem	13
10	Woman has health problem	7
11	Woman's parents want her to have an abortion	7
12	Woman was victim of rape or incest	1
13	Other reasons	6

Source: The Alan Guttmacher Institute

But laws are changing, and abortion is becoming less available. A poor woman, especially one from a rural area, may discover that she must travel several hundred miles to get to a facility that performs abortions, and she may not be able to afford either the travel or the procedure itself. What will be the result if more women are forced to have babies they do not want, cannot afford, and cannot effectively mother? From a pro-choice point of view, the inevitable result will be an ever-growing number of neglected and abused children.

However, pro-life advocates warn that if abortion is not made illegal, more and more women will choose abortion frivolously—because a child would be inconvenient or is the wrong sex, for example—and the procedure will become a form of routine birth control rather than a backup or last resort, when no other option seems possible. In fact, 40 percent of all abortions are repeat abortions. This figure has steadily grown since abortion became legalized and seems to cast doubt on whether abortion really is a procedure of "last resort."[12]

Many celebrities have recently come forward to support abortion rights. In the book *The Choices We Make*, actress and comic Whoopi Goldberg described her experience as a pregnant teenager before the 1973 legalization of abortion:

> I found out I was pregnant when I was fourteen. I didn't get a period. I talked to nobody. I panicked. I sat in hot baths. I drank these strange concoctions girls told me about—something like Johnny Walker Red with a little bit of Clorox, alcohol, baking soda. . . . I got violently ill.
>
> At that moment I was more afraid of having to explain to anybody what was wrong than of going to the park with a hanger, which is what I did. Probably I was

afraid to admit that I had had sex, because, remember, the Catholics said you only did it when you were married, and then only in the dark, and here I'd done it in the light in some hallway. But I also didn't grow up around young unmarried girls having kids.

I went to the dry cleaners and got a hanger. I took it to the park in Chelsea because it was close and had a bathroom . . . I never thought I was going to die; young people never think they're going to die. It seemed very simple at the time: You just do that, and it goes away. . . .

I didn't bleed a ton, but some. . . . Afterwards, I was in a lot of pain . . . God was with me—knock on wood—I punctured nothing; I didn't completely destroy my body.[13]

Because of the countless other women who have shared Whoopi Goldberg's experience, the symbol of a coat hanger and the phrase "back-alley abortions" often enter into pro-choice arguments. Women will always seek and have abortions, pro-choice advocates argue, so if safe, legal abortions are not available, thousands of women will die each year from unsafe or botched abortions.

Some pro-lifers claim this prediction is a "scare tactic." They insist that the day of deadly back-alley abortions is over. Why? Because the chief peril of abortion before it was legalized was infection and hemorrhaging after a sharp object punctured the **uterus.** Now legal abortions are usually done by **vacuum aspiration.** This is an inexpensive, simple method that draws the implanted egg out of the uterus.[14]

Even under the best, safest conditions, however, an abortion is more than a simple surgical procedure. The effects of the experience are different for different people, but having an abortion is often emotionally traumatic.

Sue Nathanson, in her book *Soul Crisis*, describes the "abyss of despair" into which she fell after aborting a child

Abortion was illegal when Whoopi Goldberg became pregnant at age 14. She chose a dangerous, self-inflicted, coathanger abortion.

who would have been her fourth and who was conceived despite the use of birth control. She describes herself as "committed to life, not death, having always celebrated my fertility and joy in giving birth."[15] During her time of despair, Nathanson wrote:

> Alone, I sob for myself, my child, the remains, the child smeared into bits by the vacuum aspirator, sucked from the warmth of my womb in a violent moment of death. I am a shriek of horror and anguish, straining with all my might somehow to reverse what cannot be reversed, what is irrevocable. I do not know, I cannot imagine, how I will be able to live with the horror of what is, the horror that I alone have caused.[16]

Long after her recovery from this experience, and even after deciding that she had made the right choice, Nathanson says, "[I] still wish with every ounce of my being that I could have chosen otherwise."[17]

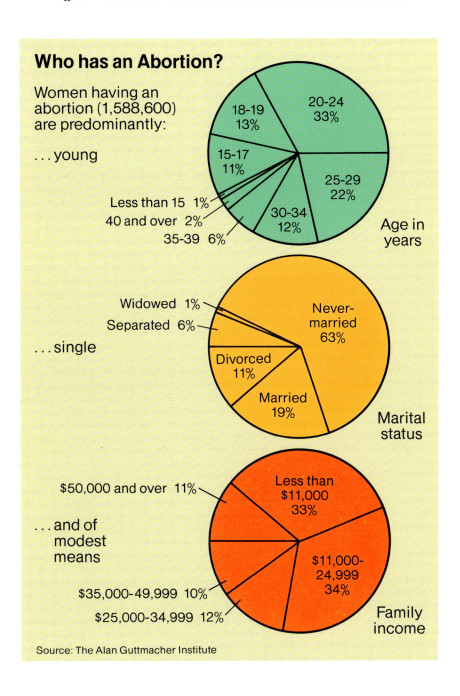

Who has an Abortion?

Women having an
abortion (1,588,600)
are predominantly:

...young

Less than 15 1%
40 and over 2%
35-39 6%

15-17
11%

18-19
13%

20-24
33%

25-29
22%

30-34
12%

Age in
years

...single

Widowed 1%
Separated 6%

Divorced
11%

Married
19%

Never-
married
63%

Marital
status

...and of
modest
means

$50,000 and over 11%

$35,000-49,999 10%

$25,000-34,999 12%

Less than
$11,000
33%

$11,000-
24,999
34%

Family
income

Source: The Alan Guttmacher Institute

Choice. This is a central concept of the abortion issue. Many women see the right to choose what happens to their own bodies—and when it happens—as a basic human right. This is especially important in cases in which pregnancy results from rape or incest, or when a teenager's life would be fundamentally altered by having a baby. Other people, however, point out that the fetus, or unborn baby, has no choice in this matter. Pro-life advocates point to other options, such as adoption, for the unwanted babies of anguished teenagers.

The debate is about more than choice, however. The issue is also about women and their roles in society, especially as contrasted with those of men. The late 1960s and early 1970s saw the emergence of the women's movement. Women began to demand the same rights and opportunities as men—in the home, in the workplace, and in government.

Abortion soon became one of the central issues in this movement. Why? Some people suspect that the real intent of laws that prohibit abortion is to control female sexuality and to restrict a woman's independence. Why, they ask, should legislators and Supreme Court justices, even the president, be allowed to tell women what to do with their own bodies?

Anti-abortionists, or pro-lifers, point to what they see as declining morality and the disintegration of the American family. They cite statistics showing that more families stayed intact when women stayed at home and raised children, and fewer children at that time got into trouble. Some pro-lifers attribute a whole array of social problems to the changes in the male/female roles and relationships that many women have fought so hard to achieve. When women have abortions because of career considerations, some pro-life advocates blame the women's movement for "murder." In short, pro-lifers often ask if women should be allowed to pay for independence, for equality, with the lives of millions of unborn children.

Not all women who consider themselves feminists, however, are pro-choice. Pro-life advocates point out that the first true feminists of the early 20th century considered abortion to be just another aspect of male domination.[18] Encouraging or, in some cases, forcing women to have abortions freed some men from the responsibility of unwanted children. A troubling report from the Alan Guttmacher Institute (an independent research group focusing on reproductive health issues) indicates that some 30 percent of women, almost one out of three, have abortions because someone else—often the man involved—wants them to.[19] Is this *choice*?

The debate about abortion will probably remain bitter and divisive for some time. As sociologist Kristin Luker says in her book *Abortion and the Politics of Motherhood*, "Beliefs about the rightness or wrongness of abortion both represent and illuminate our most cherished beliefs about the world, about motherhood, and about what it means to be human. It should not surprise us that these views admit of very little compromise."[20] The abortion debate is not so much an argument about facts as it is one about what certain facts mean and how we should assess them.

Dr. Bernard Nathanson, narrator of a film called The Silent Scream, *illustrates the development of a fetus.*

WHEN DOES LIFE BEGIN?

Jane Doe is 15 years old and pregnant. She goes to a counseling center she has seen advertised as helping teenagers "in trouble."

"Let me show you something before we begin talking," says her counselor, and Jane finds herself staring in horror at a television screen. Through advanced sonographic techniques, a film called the *The Silent Scream*, narrated by Dr. Bernard Nathanson, shows the outline of a fetus in the uterus of an unknown woman who is supposedly 12 weeks pregnant. As a suction device approaches, the fetus moves frantically, appearing to thrash around to escape the device, but there is no escape. The head is crushed, and the limbs are torn away. Then the device sucks out the remains.

According to Nathanson, who performed more than 60,000 abortions but is now staunchly pro-life, if you watch this film you can see the baby's mouth "open in a silent scream." You can't ignore the agitation that follows—the increased heartbeat and breathing and the rapidly moving limbs of the fetus. "So there is no question," Dr. Nathanson says in the film, that "this child feels pain and actually senses danger."

Made in 1985, *The Silent Scream* has been viewed by thousands in the medical field. As a result, many viewers decided not to perform any more abortions. The film has also been shown in counseling clinics to many women and to girls like Jane who are contemplating abortion. The effect is often similar—the women cannot proceed with their abortions.

Showing such a film to women troubled by their pregnancies enrages pro-choice supporters. Many dispute the age of the fetus and even disagree about what, exactly, the film shows because the view is not totally clear. Pro-choice counselors offer a different video depicting what they call a more typical abortion (similar to more than 90 percent of the procedures). This film lasts 84 seconds and shows two aborted embryos amounting to about two tablespoons of blood and tissue.[1]

The images in *The Silent Scream*, however, are difficult to forget. The questions these images raise about abortion are more difficult to answer now than in the past, when technology was unable to provide a view of life within the uterus.

Is abortion, in fact, painful to the fetus? And, more to the point, does the procedure involve taking a human life, therefore making it murder? Such inquiries provide no immediate, obvious answers because they are part of a larger question—the one asked most often in any debate about abortion—"When does life begin?"

Because the outrage over murder is almost always reserved for the killing of humans, perhaps the question needs to be more specific: "When does *human* life begin?" Killing a chimpanzee, our closest biological relative, angers animal rights activists, but most people do not consider it murder. If the term *murder* only applies to human beings, when does the fetus become a person, a human being? When *does* human life begin?

For pro-life advocates, the answer is "at conception"—when the woman's egg has been fertilized by the man's sperm. In a 1989 landmark case, *Webster v. Reproductive Health Services*, the United States Supreme Court upheld a Missouri fetal rights law that asserts that "life begins at conception." Because this Supreme Court decision leaves abortion restrictions up to individual states, the ruling has had enormous impact on the abortion debate.

In spite of the wording in the *Webster* decision, however, many scientists point out that "life" actually begins long *before* conception. The human egg and the sperm are each alive on their own. Destroying either of them (something that happens when women menstruate and when men ejaculate) is certainly not considered murder. But does the union of egg and sperm suddenly, with certainty, produce human life?

Dr. Jerome Lejeune, an expert in genetics, says that at the moment of fertilization, "each of us has a very precise starting moment which is the time at which the whole necessary and sufficient genetic information is gathered inside one cell, the fertilized egg." The amount of information about each new individual contained in the fertilized egg is so great, Dr. Lejeune says, that more than five sets (*not volumes*) of the *Encyclopedia Britannica* would be required to store it all.[2]

Even some people who favor the pro-choice viewpoint believe that life probably begins at conception. They do not, however, give the fetus the same rights as those of the

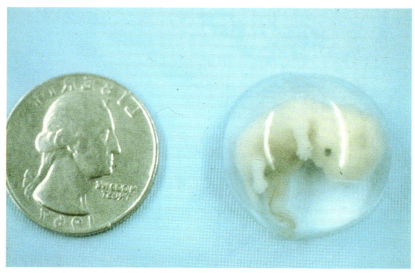

This five-week-old fetus is approximately the size of a quarter. It could not survive outside the uterus.

pregnant woman. How can one life have more value than another? Viewing a fetus as a "potential" or "developing" life provides one answer.

Geneticist Charles A. Gardner says that the fertilized egg is not a complete, "prepackaged human being." He points out that the fertilized egg can take many different paths depending on "chance events" within the uterus as the embryo develops. "The information required to make an eye or a finger," Gardner says, "does not exist in the fertilized egg. It exists in the positions and interactions of cells and molecules that will be formed only at a later time." In fact Gardner claims that scientists cannot distinguish, in any significant way, early human embryos from early mouse embryos.[3]

This claim does not make the fertilized egg sound very significant. But one difficulty in the pro-choice argument is

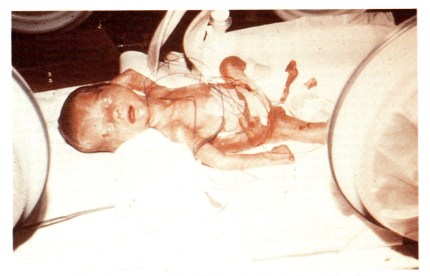

After 21 weeks in utero, this child is being kept alive with a life-support system. It could not survive on its own.

that almost everyone agrees that abortions should not be performed for such a frivolous reason as a planned vacation. If some reasons don't justify an abortion, then wouldn't the developing fetus seem to have some recognizable value? Is the fetus of *less* value than the mother?

One of the most effective ways to argue either side of the abortion question is to look closely at what is taking place inside the uterus of a pregnant woman. Each human being starts out about the size of the period at the end of this sentence. Sperm and egg unite; one cell becomes two; two become four; and so on. By the sixth day, the fertilized egg finds a place in the uterus where it can attach itself and grow.[4]

Beyond this point, however, the way in which fetal development is described seems to depend on one's position on the abortion question. Most pro-life supporters believe

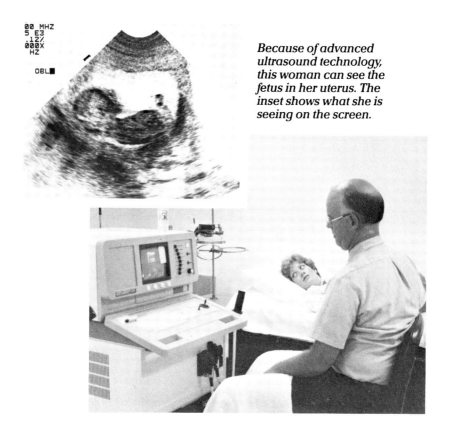

Because of advanced ultrasound technology, this woman can see the fetus in her uterus. The inset shows what she is seeing on the screen.

an embryo contains a "complex genetic blueprint for every detail of human development."[5] In other words, they believe that the embryo contains the future physical characteristics of the child. Abortion-rights supporters, however, tend to emphasize how *un*human the embryo of the first few weeks appears—first, worm-like, then like a fish or amphibian, with parts resembling gills and a tail.[6]

The heart begins to beat before the end of the first month, and pro-life supporters recognize the rudiments of the brain, spinal cord, and nervous system at this point.[7] On the other hand, pro-choice supporters say that human body parts are barely recognizable until after the second month. They further argue that brain activity–recognizably *human* brain activity–begins around the middle of the seventh month.[8] Pro-lifers, however, say that doctors can detect brain waves at 40 days and that the brain controls much of the activity of the fetus by the time it is six weeks old.[9]

Even **viability**–the point at which a baby can survive outside the mother's womb–appears to be in question. Many in the medical community say that a baby reaches its earliest possible stage of viability at approximately 24 weeks. Before this the lungs of the fetus are not adequately developed to carry on alone or even with artificial means. Therefore the fetus is not viable; it cannot survive outside the mother's womb.[10] But at least one pro-life publication claims that babies born at 19 or 20 weeks have survived.[11] However, many scientists believe that at this point (between 19 and 24

A group of pro-lifers conducted a burial service for 13 aborted fetuses in Minneapolis, Minnesota, in 1987.

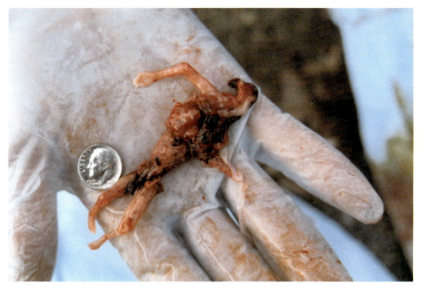

An eight-week-old aborted fetus

weeks), the fetal brain does not yet have the capacity for human thought.[12]

So a new question emerges: What determines the point at which a fetus becomes a human being—the capability of thought, feelings, viability, or something else? Many people try to answer questions about the beginning of life by locating a human fetus on a continuum stretching from the single sex cell to a human newborn. These people maintain

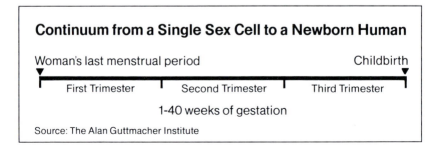

Continuum from a Single Sex Cell to a Newborn Human

Woman's last menstrual period   Childbirth

First Trimester   Second Trimester   Third Trimester

1-40 weeks of gestation

Source: The Alan Guttmacher Institute

that the way we look at a developing human depends on where it is on the continuum.

If the fetus is far enough along this continuum to be treated as the human person it may become, then to deliberately end its life is clearly murder. If the fetus is in its early development, however, and not fully formed, "then whatever rights it has are more similar to those of the fertilized egg it once was than to the baby it may become; to end its life is therefore something closer on the moral scale to **contraception** than to murder."[13]

On this continuum, many pro-choice advocates mark the end of the third month (the first trimester) as significant. This is the period during which simple, routine abortions most often take place. The end of the sixth month (second trimester) is also significant because after 24 weeks (the stage of viability), abortions become more complicated and risky. They are also being performed on fetuses that might be able to survive outside the mother's womb.

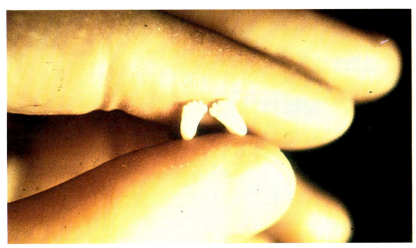

The feet of a fetus that is about 10 weeks old

Pro-life advocates see this continuum approach as inevitably leading to a "slippery slope." Once a person grants meaningful life to a fetus at 24 weeks (because of viability), what about the fetus that is just a few days shy of that? Even more appalling to pro-lifers is the following question: If life begins at birth, should women be able to legally abort babies one week, one day, one hour before labor begins? Only a few decades ago, before incubators, babies born at seven months (30 weeks) were not viable. Was aborting babies at seven months okay then, but not now—simply because of a mechanical invention?

Perhaps the most simple, clear-cut answer to the question of when human life begins is "at conception." But if that is true, why don't we add those nine months in utero to our ages? This suggestion is not as crazy as it might sound. The tradition in China is to consider a person a year old at birth because of the months spent in the womb.[14]

Other, more crucial questions raised by the concept of human life beginning at conception are in the area of fetal rights. If we recognize and value a fetus as a person, then a fetus must have the rights of any other person. But to what extent?

Due in part to the *Webster* decision of 1989, a Tennessee court ruled that the seven frozen embryos being fought over by a divorcing couple were "human beings existing as embryos." The judge gave custody of the embryos to the mother.[15]

In such a case, if a woman chose to have an embryo injected into her uterus some time in the future, and it resulted in a pregnancy, could the man who "fathered" the embryos be considered responsible for the children produced from them? Would those children have the same

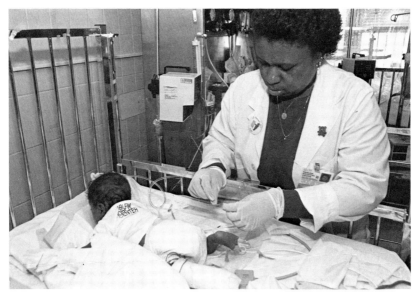

A nurse at Harlem Hospital takes a blood sample from a baby who was born with AIDS.

legal rights as any children the couple might have had while they were together? What if the woman chose not to have the embryos implanted in her womb? Wouldn't disposing of them be murder according to the court's ruling?

On June 1, 1992, the Tennessee Supreme Court overturned the ruling of the lower court with its decision that a divorced man cannot be forced to become a father through the use of frozen embryos. Arthur Caplan, director of the Center for Biomedical Ethics at the University of Minnesota, pointed out that "in this case the court said that a man cannot be made to become a parent against his will. This raises the question as to whether other courts would be willing to compel women to do what this court is not willing to compel a man to do [become a parent against her will]." Caplan added that it is sometimes said that if men could have children, abortion would be a right. "This case illustrates that that may not be as apocryphal a statement as we might have thought it was," he said.[16]

Another question reveals additional complexities involved in fetal rights: Do law-enforcement agencies have the duty to protect a fetus from its own mother? In several recent cases in different states, women have been arrested and charged with child abuse for taking drugs or for drinking alcohol while they were pregnant. A few have been imprisoned.

Society can argue that whatever is needed—even imprisonment—to get a pregnant woman off drugs is justifiable because of all the drug-addicted and irreparably harmed babies who are being born to such women. However, the courts apparently do not see the necessity of protecting a fetus from its father who has endangered its life by beating his pregnant wife. The inconsistency of such laws and the

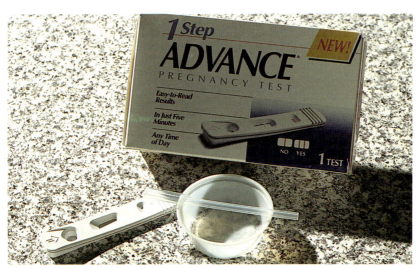

Home pregnancy tests allow easy, early detection.

For those considering an abortion, the decision is one of the most difficult and distressing choices a woman will ever make.

difficulties of enforcing them make fetal rights a troubling and cloudy part of the abortion debate.[17]

The issues surrounding abortion have not always been so complex. Only recently has it been possible to look directly at a developing fetus inside a woman's body. This firsthand look changed the debate forever. Until 50 years ago, a woman did not even know for certain that she was pregnant until the baby began to move inside the womb—during the fifth or sixth month. Once fetuses were no longer "invisible," and once early detection of pregnancy became routine, defining the status of a fetus became much more urgent because of the potential effect on abortion laws.

WOMANHOOD AND MOTHERHOOD

The sensation feels something like a butterfly—small, papery, fluttering wings—caught inside the abdomen. Commonly called "quickening," the first detectable movement of a fetus is something no woman can adequately describe. Nor is she likely ever to forget it.

Until pregnancy tests were developed about 50 years ago, a woman didn't know for sure that she was pregnant until quickening occurred during the fifth or sixth month of pregnancy. The ability to detect pregnancy shortly after conception is only one of several technological advances that have changed women's lives in recent years. The development of the contraceptive pill, and easier and safer abortion methods, have allowed women to plan their pregnancies and to schedule them in relation to other goals and dreams.

Such technological advances, combined with an increase in opportunities for women in the workplace, have allowed the role of "career woman" to gain more and more prestige in American society. More than ever before, a woman can have status and glamour in her life without marriage and children. But many people equate the emergence of the career woman with a devaluation of the roles of wife and mother.

According to sociologist Kristin Luker, extensive interviews with a wide range of women show that "the major social significance of this change has been the creation of a chasm between women who have options outside the family and women who do not."[1]

Despite the fact that many women work outside the home because of necessity (they support or share in the support of their families), some pro-life advocates maintain that social change and technological advances have allowed women to place career or other considerations above childbearing. For pro-choice advocates, these social changes and techno-logical advances have given each woman more options from which to choose. As a result, the question of equality between men and women is being closely examined.

Many young women choose to have professional careers, and they prepare for high-level business positions.

*With an increasing number of women working outside the home—
by choice or necessity—day care is a way of life for many children.*

Discussing the equality of the sexes, however, always
involves one exception—only women can bear children.
And motherhood is clearly more than sustaining a growing
fetus and then birthing it nine months later. Therefore, any
discussion of abortion must go beyond the question of the
fetus to look at what it means to be a modern woman—a
woman who can choose whether or not to become a mother.

In *The Way of All Women*, Esther Harding discusses her
ideas about the "maternal instinct" and the emotional and
psychological effects of abortion:

> Any other minor operation is an experience which can
> be accepted at its face value, and after the pain, anxiety
> and convalescence are over it falls into the background,
> leaving no long train of inner consequences. But an
> interference with pregnancy does not act this way, for
> pregnancy involves more than physical changes. The
> bearing of children is a biological task. The roots of the
> maternal instinct reach back into the deepest layers of

a woman's nature, touching forces of which she may be profoundly unconscious. When a woman becomes pregnant these ancient powers stir within her, whether she knows it or not, and she disregards them only at her peril.[2]

Another author, Kathryn Allen Rabuzzi, describes abortion as "a kind of amputation" that "removes something whose existence simultaneously threatens yet forms a new part of a woman's very selfhood."[3]

Proponents on both sides of the abortion debate seem to agree that abortions cannot be taken lightly. Abortion can be quite difficult for women to endure emotionally. Pro-life advocates view this emotional trauma as part of the argument against legalizing the procedure. But abortion-rights activists respond with a question: "Because of the trauma involved, how can anyone claim—as some pro-lifers do—that abortion is being used as 'easy' birth control?"

Although men are seldom mentioned in this debate, the father of an unborn child is often affected by a decision to abort. Many pro-choice supporters argue that since the woman bears the child, whether or not to abort should be her decision. But the father has also played a key role in the process and may want to be included in the decision-making process.

Abortion is a difficult decision not only because of the moral issues involved, but also because of what motherhood involves. This heightens the emotional content of the debate, especially among women with differing views.

Given an array of lifestyle choices, most people choose one that seems valid and fulfilling to them. One woman may become a pro-life activist because she views child-bearing and family values as central to her life. Another woman may become a pro-choice activist because she feels that planning when to bear a child, fighting for an equal role in society, and struggling for personal freedom and self-determination are crucial to *her* life. These two women will probably make different choices. Society, however, may demand that each represent and defend an entire philosophy that includes questions about the sanctity of life, about "the place women should occupy in society, and about what the proper family structure should be."[4]

Some pro-choice advocates see reproductive freedom as necessary for equality, especially in the workplace. They point to blatant evidence of discrimination against women because employers consider them continually "at risk" of getting pregnant and then leaving their jobs. As author Grace Paley puts it, "What [men] really want to do is take back ownership of women's bodies. They want to return us to a time when even our children weren't our own; we were simply the receptacles to have these children."[5]

Not all feminists, however, are pro-choice. Many pro-lifers feel strongly about, and work toward, equality for women. Others say they are pro-life because "true liberation begins when we renounce means that kill. The taking of human life as a solution to human problems stems from some of the worst masculine delusions that afflict society."[6]

Pro-life feminists often question why any child, unwanted or otherwise, should automatically be seen as an obstacle to a woman's fulfillment. What, they ask, does that attitude say about the value of children, of human life in general? And they regret that the women's movement, so often characterized by compassion for minorities and others who are treated unjustly by society, should care so little about the most marginal of all—the unborn.[7]

CRUSADERS FOR "LIFE" AND FOR "CHOICE"

The disfigured fetus was aborted nearly two years ago during the 19th week of pregnancy. Called "Baby Choice" by members of Operation Rescue, the fetus is used by these anti-abortion crusaders to shocking effect. Most of the time, Baby Choice floats in a jar of formaldehyde. However, when the group's controversial leader, Randall Terry, holds a press conference, he often displays the fetus in a tiny coffin lined with white satin. "That's not just a blob of cells," proclaims Terry. "That's a little girl." [1]

Since 1987, Terry has turned a small band of anti-abortion radicals in Binghamton, New York, into the fastest-growing wing of the pro-life movement. In 1989 Terry claimed that his demonstrators had "saved" between 140 and 350 babies and that number was steadily growing. [2]

How does this group operate? Randall Terry, a former used-car salesman, is a fiery speaker who travels around the country to activate conservative church groups. He promotes "rescues" in which the demonstrators lie down around an abortion clinic to form a human blockade. Women who want to enter the building are met by "sidewalk counselors" who try to persuade them against having an abortion. When the police arrive, the demonstrators go limp and are carted off to jail.[3]

Some radical anti-abortion activists also promote different forms of "physical intervention," including property destruction, harassment, assault of clinic staffs, and even death threats. Such violence has increased steadily since 1983.[4] In fact, in one protest led by Terry, an unborn child was inadvertently a victim when a demonstrator punched a pregnant clinic worker in the stomach—an act that caused the woman to miscarry.[5]

Terry claims that Operation Rescue does not condone or advocate violence. He urges his followers to be arrested by the hundreds. By doing this, he hopes to win the sympathy

Police arrest a man for blocking the entrance of a clinic that offers abortion services in St. Louis Park, a suburb of Minneapolis.

of the nation in the same way that the civil rights movement did during the 1950s and 1960s. However, any identification of pro-life radicals with civil rights demonstrators angers their opponents. Pro-choice advocates think the difference is obvious: "blocking access to abortion clinics is not much different from blocking access to schools, voting booths, and public accommodations."[6]

In one confrontation, a young black woman approached an abortion clinic for counseling about her pregnancy. She asked a group of pro-choice volunteers for an escort to avoid any trouble when entering the building. Pro-life protesters were blocking the entrance, carrying graphic pictures of mutilated infants, and were questioning women about their intentions to "murder their own babies."

In 1984 a bomb ripped through this abortion clinic in Wheaton, Maryland. The clinic had been the target of a weekend protest by members of the Pro-life Nonviolent Action Project.

Pro-life activist Randall Terry read from the Bible when he addressed Operation Rescue supporters in Wichita, Kansas.

The young woman stayed calm until a young man began shouting charges at her that the great civil rights leader Martin Luther King, Jr., would "turn over in his grave for what she was doing" and that her actions were contributing to the genocide, or deliberate destruction, of African Americans.

According to an observer, the woman's composure gave way to rage as she "stared him in his eyes with tears in hers, then quietly and coolly said, 'You're a white boy, and you don't give a damn thing about me, who I am or what I do. And you know even less about Martin Luther King or being black. What you have to say to me means nothin', not a damn thing.' He was silenced and she walked on."[7] Such encounters, with or without racial overtones, typically occur every day at clinics all over the country.

During the first 70 years of the 20th century, abortion decisions were primarily in the hands of physicians. A doctor could perform the procedure legally as long as, in his opinion, the abortion was needed to preserve the life of the mother. But such "preservation" was widely defined to include many questionable emotional and psychological disturbances caused by pregnancy.[8]

Wealthier and more powerful families had few problems obtaining abortions; poorer women or those who simply could not make the necessary medical connections had to accept their pregnancies or resort to dangerous, self-induced or illegal abortions. Police arrested and prosecuted many "criminal abortionists," but others flourished. Physicians could claim that they performed any individual abortion legally—to protect the life of the mother.[9]

The battle for abortion reform began in the 1960s, about the same time as the women's movement began. In most states, reform was being achieved by giving physicians more and more leeway to perform abortions at their discretion.

Pro-life activists block the doors to a clinic in Washington, D.C.

Clinic volunteers lock arms and shield a patient with an umbrella as they escort her to the entrance of a clinic in Atlanta, Georgia.

At many clinics, pro-life activists do "sidewalk counseling" in an attempt to stop women who are going in for an abortion.

But some activists in the women's movement wanted more than reform. They wanted abortion laws repealed–a move that would remove all restrictions on abortion. Why? Because claiming that women had a *right* to abortion challenged the male-dominated medical profession's control of the abortion decision.[10]

In 1973 the *Roe v. Wade* ruling granted women the legal right to choose abortion. Feeling reassured by this landmark Supreme Court decision, abortion rights activists felt secure enough to retire from action. The pro-life movement, however, was shocked by the *Roe* decision and took belated action.

For the next 10 years, efforts by the pro-life movement aroused little response. Americans weren't interested in the debate, which the Supreme Court seemed to have settled. Because of the occasional outbursts of violence against abortion clinics during the 1970s, the pro-life movement seemed too radical for most Americans.

During the early 1980s, however, pro-life groups reshaped their image into something more middle-of-the-road. They began using more women–rather than white males–as spokespersons. They softened their views on abortion in cases of rape and incest and tried to avoid alienating feminists. Pro-life activists shifted the focus of the debate from the rights of women to the rights of the fetus. Still, most Americans remained indifferent.[11]

In the late 1980s, the abortion debate began to take center stage in American life, due to such groups as Terry's Operation Rescue and some other Christian fundamentalist groups. They emphasized how babylike the fetus is, used modern technology to "prove" the humanity of the fetus, and appealed to the public's tender feelings toward babies.[12]

Finally, people began to pay attention and even accept what the pro-lifers were saying—that women were acting irresponsibly, and that a million-and-a-half "unborn children" were being "destroyed" each year.[13]

At the center of the abortion debate now is a "new breed of protester." These activists are stronger, more aggressive, and more determined than in the past.[14] In 1988, for example, the Reverend Norman Weslin, a Roman Catholic priest and retired U.S. Army officer, founded an organization called the Lambs of Christ. Although a small group with only about 30 full-time and 250 part-time workers, the Lambs have become a major force in the abortion battle.[15]

These activists travel from clinic to clinic, and usually from jail to jail, throughout the United States. They often stake out the neighborhood of a doctor who works in an abortion clinic and inform everyone who will listen that the doctor is a "baby killer." The Lambs also harass and threaten the clinic staff and the doctor's family. When a doctor receives death threats, when his or her children are followed to and from school, and when the doctor's clinic is repeatedly set on fire, it becomes difficult to continue providing abortions in the area. In this way, the Lambs and other extremist groups have steadily and dramatically diminished the availability of abortion.

Although most pro-life advocates would never resort to such extreme methods, they do share a common goal—to close as many abortion clinics as possible. In response to pro-life toughness, including violence or threatened violence, some pro-choice activists have also taken extreme action. On the West Coast, for example, a group of women broke into churches frequented by pro-life advocates and painted pro-choice slogans on the walls.[16]

The Religious Coalition for Abortion Rights staffs a booth at the Michigan State Fair.

This pro-life advocate is distributing anti-abortion literature in a St. Paul, Minnesota, neighborhood located near a clinic that provides abortions.

Many pro-choice activists have organized to defend abortion clinics physically, and they openly confront pro-life "rescuers" and sidewalk counselors. Compare the confrontation in Wichita, Kansas, during the summer of 1991 with the one in Buffalo, New York, less than a year later.

Operation Rescue organized both protests in an attempt to block access to abortion clinics and gain public awareness. In Wichita thousands of pro-life activists succeeded in disrupting clinic activity for several weeks. In Buffalo, however, the protests fizzled. The pro-life activists were more than matched by those on the pro-choice side. Buffalo also showed how ugly both sides could become. Pro-choice demonstrators didn't just form human barricades to protect the clinics; they also spat at, punched, and screamed obscenities at pro-life demonstrators. In response, a pro-life leader displayed a 20-week-old "aborted" fetus that had, in fact, been stillborn.[17]

Other pro-choice supporters have chosen a more political route by pledging to make abortion an issue in every election. Their support for candidates in local, state, and national elections often hinges on the candidate's position on a single question: "Do women have the right to choose abortion?" Protesters on both sides of the issue become most vocal during election years. In April 1992, an estimated half-million abortion rights supporters (the largest group that has demonstrated in the nation's capital) marched on Washington, D.C. Sometimes the pro-choice movement wins support by simply publicizing the extreme tactics of certain pro-life groups. Even some of the older anti-abortion organizations, such as the National Right to Life Committee, want nothing to do with Operation Rescue, Lambs of Christ, and other extremist groups.[18]

Thousands of pro-choice supporters attended a rally in New York City.

What many people find difficult to understand is that some pro-life advocates oppose not only abortion but also contraception and sex education. Randall Terry has been quoted as saying, "I don't think Christians should use birth control. You consummate your marriage as often as you like—and if you have babies, you have babies."[19]

An opinion that seems to be widely held across the country is well stated by a New Mexico nurse: "I just wish that even half the righteousness and energy that's gone into fighting school-based clinics, condoms, and abortion had gone into fighting ignorance, poverty, and no health care. That's my idea of pro-life."[20]

Some people question the sincerity of pro-lifers who seem more intent on political goals than on social ones. For instance, why don't pro-life activists set up an operation to rescue babies before they die as a result of poor prenatal care, or to help children who are mistreated by their overwhelmed, reluctant parents? In one community, some activists who called themselves "pro-life" opposed a group home for babies with AIDS.[21] Don't these social issues involving babies need the same sort of support as the abortion issue?

However, the pro-choice side also has its share of extremists. In the 1950s and 1960s, the pro-choice movement prided itself on being careful of and open to larger concerns. It now runs the risk of becoming narrow and rigid. Some pro-choice leaders focus almost entirely on a woman's right to an abortion without regard for the reasons for, or the consequences of, abortion. Such a narrow focus ignores the moral complexities of abortion and fails to recognize that the American public does not support the right to abortion under any and all circumstances.[22]

In a 1990 essay about the ethics of choice, writer and editor Daniel Callahan (who is pro-choice) deplores the fact that:

> Much less is heard about the social harm of unwanted pregnancies, much less about the terrible and tragic choice posed by an abortion, much less about the moral nature of the choice, and practically nothing about the need to reduce the number of abortions.... No number of abortions seems to be too many. It is as if, in face of the pro-life movement, some feminist leaders have decided to be as single-minded and unmeasured as their opponents.[23]

Ultimately, perhaps neither side addresses the issue in a way that is personal enough to help women through the crisis of an unwanted pregnancy. After dealing with her inner conflict over her own abortion, Sue Nathanson says in *Soul Crisis*:

> Pro-choice advocates perceive the woman who communicates her sense of guilt and despair to be out of touch with her own needs, either deficient in feminist consciousness or victimized by Right-to-Life propaganda. Right-to-Life advocates perceive the woman who displays no feelings as either inhuman or insensitive or as a victim of a culture that permits her to be indifferent to the value of life and provides her with no other options. Where, in this culture, can I possibly find a mirror of my subjective experience?[24]

THE MORALITY
OF ABORTION

*"For those who say I can't impose my morality on others,
I say just watch me."*
    —Joseph Scheidler
       Executive Director of Pro-Life Action League[1]

*"See, when you do something like that [have an abor-
tion], you do it because for you it is your only choice.
The sad thing is you really want to be able to feel bad
about it without feeling wrong."*
    —Kathy Najimy
       Actress, director, and writer[2]

Morality relates to principles of right and wrong. The
moral issues involved in the abortion debate are among the
most difficult to settle. Judging something as morally right
or wrong makes it seem clear and uncomplicated. Most
pro-life advocates think abortion is wrong. To them, it is
murder. Many pro-life advocates admit that abortion might
be acceptable under certain circumstances—primarily if the
pregnancy would prove fatal to the mother. Some pro-lifers
even make an exception in cases of incest and rape.

The problem with making exceptions, however, is that it raises some troubling questions: Why should the right to life depend on the *circumstances* of conception? And if exceptions are extended to one fetus, why should they be withheld from other fetuses?[3]

Public opinion polls show that most Americans do not see all personal reasons for abortion as equally valid, and they express great uncertainty over the morality of abortion. Using this sense of uncertainty, the pro-life movement has brought to the surface many doubts and qualms not always addressed by the pro-choice movement. For many people, abortion threatens whatever safeguards we have erected against arbitrary and abusive power of one person over the life or death of another. Does anyone have the right to devalue the human life of another? Is *unwanted* the same as *valueless?* Because a child is unwanted, is it of no value?[4]

As Daniel Callahan points out, "If, for some people, to have choice is itself the beginning and end of morality, for most people it is just the beginning. It does not end until a supportable, justifiable choice has been made, one that can be judged right or wrong by the individual herself based on some reasonably serious, not patently self-interested way of thinking about ethics."[5]

Many people think that the pro-choice view represents a "feel good" kind of morality—"If it feels good, do it, no matter whom it hurts."[6] Not all abortions are requested because of the age or marital status of the woman or because of poverty, rape, or fetal deformity. Sometimes women choose abortion simply because pregnancy would be inconvenient. Some pro-life advocates accuse pro-choice groups of minimizing the experience of abortion, implying it's little different from "getting a tooth pulled or a wart removed."[7]

A growing number of *feminist* pro-lifers are effectively confronting their pro-choice counterparts for whom choice, freedom, and independence are so important. Legal abortion, pro-lifers point out, gives men a "potent new weapon in the old business of manipulating and abandoning women."[8] These pro-life feminists claim that pro-choice arguments do not always address the reality of *coerced* abortions. Many women—especially if they are young, poor, and black—feel that men have forced them into having an abortion. If so, what choice did they have?

Pro-choice advocates also talk about morality. They ask, How moral is it to bring more unwanted and uncared-for children into the world? How moral is it to force a young girl to go through a pregnancy (and perhaps a high-risk delivery) resulting from rape or incest? Is preventing the birth of a severely deformed, seriously ill, or drug-addicted baby really immoral? After great suffering, the baby would probably soon die anyway.

Kenneth S. Kantzer, writing for *Christianity Today*, calls on pro-lifers to:

> Give us assurance that you are prepared for the consequences of a strict law against abortion. Tens of thousands now aborted would be brought to term. . . . Will the church lead the way in providing support to those troubled families? . . . Are we willing to make the sacrifices, emotional as well as financial, that will be required to welcome them into the human family and provide for their needs. If we cannot respond with an unblinking "yes" to these questions, we have no right on moral grounds to oppose their abortions.[9]

Pro-choice advocates also wonder how much of society's moral indignation relates to abortion being considered murder and how much really reflects society's ambivalence about sexuality, female sexuality in particular. This question may be especially relevant for pro-lifers who are also against birth control and sex education. Perhaps their agenda has less to do with the rights of the unborn than with their beliefs that sexuality, outside of marriage, without intent to reproduce, is morally wrong.

Access to abortion increased during the 1970s and early 1980s, while at the same time resources for poor families diminished. This may be due to many factors but, as Callahan says: "Is it wholly an accident that our country combines the world's most liberal abortion laws with the poorest social support systems for women, mothers, and children?"[10]

Pro-choice supporters ask pro-lifers if they will take responsibility for the lives they want to save and for the needs of women and children. This family, for example, is homeless.

Births Out of Wedlock

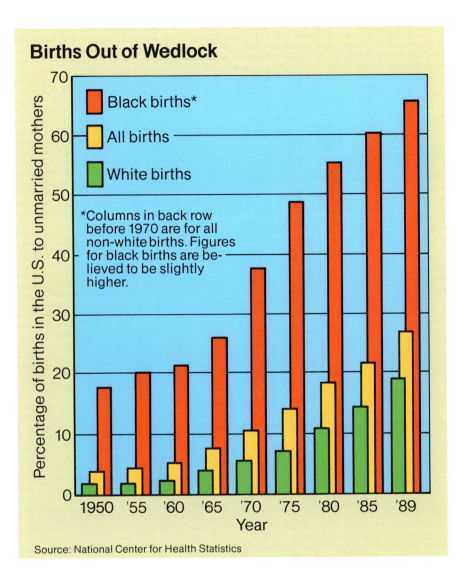

Source: National Center for Health Statistics

Similarly, sociologist James R. Kelly points out that, "Freedom requires more than one true option. Society must provide women enough help so that no one feels she has no choice but abortion."[11]

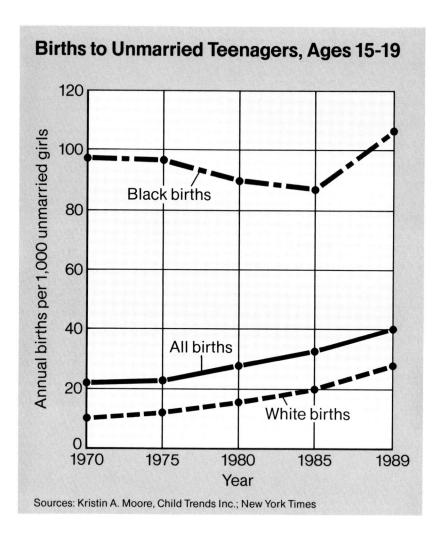

Births to Unmarried Teenagers, Ages 15-19

Sources: Kristin A. Moore, Child Trends Inc.; New York Times

Some people on both sides of the abortion debate would like to see a guarantee that any gains for the unborn fetus would coincide with gains for women—gains such as adequate health benefits (especially for prenatal and infant care), housing, child care, job protection, and drug treatment.[12]

In recent years, medical researchers have raised questions about the use of **fetal tissue** to treat certain diseases. Using body parts and tissue from aborted fetuses has shown promising results in the treatment of such widespread diseases as Parkinson's, Alzheimer's, and diabetes. However, fetal tissue from spontaneous abortions **(miscarriages)** does not appear to be as serviceable as that from induced abortions, because a miscarried (stillborn) fetus has often been dead too long for its tissue to be useful. Many pro-choice advocates believe that fetal tissue from aborted fetuses should be used to improve the health of suffering people.

Most pro-life advocates think using fetal tissue resembles experiments done by the Nazis during World War II, when they tortured and killed prisoners in the name of medical research. The administrations of Ronald Reagan and George Bush, both pro-life presidents, have placed federal restrictions on fetal-tissue research.

Could such research influence a woman's decision to have an abortion? Would some women get pregnant and then abort in order to save the life of a loved one? Could fetal tissue be bought and sold? Most researchers insist that abuses can easily be avoided. Others point out that when a woman is agonizing over an abortion decision, the last thing on her mind is where the fetal parts will go. In an article for *America*, however, Stephen G. Post points out that the fetal tissue debate detracts from the goal of preventing abortions. He is haunted by the prospect of a society whose "medical institutions are inextricably bound up with elective abortions and whose people come to believe that for their own health they have every right to feed off the unborn."[13]

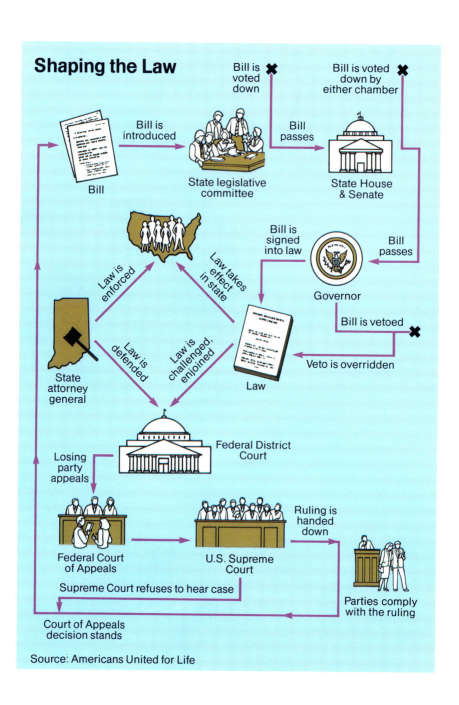

Shaping the Law

Bill is voted down ✖

Bill is voted down by either chamber ✖

Bill is introduced

Bill

State legislative committee

Bill passes

Bill passes

State House & Senate

Law is enforced

Law takes effect in state

Bill is signed into law

Governor

Law is defended

Law is challenged, enjoined

State attorney general

Law

Bill is vetoed ✖

Veto is overridden

Losing party appeals

Federal District Court

Federal Court of Appeals

U.S. Supreme Court

Ruling is handed down

Supreme Court refuses to hear case

Parties comply with the ruling

Court of Appeals decision stands

Source: Americans United for Life

ROE v. WADE

Laws regarding abortion rights tend to change over time—sometimes gradually, sometimes dramatically. How does this happen? Primarily, these changes occur because men and women with differing stands on abortion get elected to public office or are appointed to the Supreme Court by the president. Elected officials reflect their views in the laws they pass, and justices in the way they interpret laws—in their rulings, or decisions.

When a group or an individual challenges a state law, the case can go all the way to the U.S. Supreme Court. The Court then makes a final decision. In this way, one person can begin the process that sets legal precedent and affects the nation as a whole. This is exactly what happened on January 22, 1973, when the Supreme Court handed down its decision in the case of *Roe v. Wade*.

For about 100 years preceding the *Roe* ruling, each state legislature had been solely responsible for deciding when and if abortion was legal; but abortion laws underwent reform during the 1960s. The legal argument for reform asserted that existing laws against abortion took away a

The 1973 Supreme Court from left to right: Justices Potter Stewart, Lewis F. Powell, Jr., William O. Douglas, Thurgood Marshall, Warren E. Burger (Chief Justice), Harry A. Blackmun, William J. Brennan, Jr., William H. Rehnquist, Byron R. White. The Roe v. Wade *decision affected abortion laws in 31 states.*

woman's constitutional right of personal privacy. Advocates of abortion-law reform also claimed that a fetus had never been considered a person in the eyes of the law. As proof of this claim, they pointed out that an individual who causes a woman to miscarry is charged with assault, not murder.[1]

Into this legal turmoil walked a poor, single woman named Norma McCorvey, alias "Jane Roe." She lived in Texas, which had one of the most restrictive laws against abortion. Jane Roe could have gotten an abortion legally in California, but she could not afford to go there. Because Roe's predicament was so typical of other women who had considered or sought abortions, she became their symbol and seemed to represent them. Henry Wade, the district attorney of Dallas County, was responsible for enforcing the law in the area where Roe lived. Thus the case became *Roe v. Wade*.[2]

Abortion-rights groups, supplying expert legal help, became involved in the case. The *Roe* case also coincided with the growing strength of the abortion-reform movement, and the case came before a liberal Supreme Court.

The *Roe v. Wade* ruling struck down all existing state laws restricting abortion and created a new law for the entire nation. The Court ruled that the "due process" clause of the 14th Amendment bars a state from prohibiting abortion."[3] (The 14th Amendment says that "No state shall make or enforce any law which shall abridge the privileges or immunities of a person of life, liberty, or property, without due process of law.") The phrase "due process of law" forbids the states to violate most rights protected by the Bill of Rights.

Jane Roe claimed that Texas, by enforcing its anti-abortion law, deprived her of "liberty" without due process of law. Liberty, she claimed, included the freedom to have an abortion. In *The Court and the Constitution*, Archibald Cox writes that "it is hard to think of a more fundamental invasion of personal liberty than to tell a woman that she must or may not bear a child. Her whole life—physical, psychological, spiritual, familial, and economic—will be profoundly affected. Would not just about everyone agree that this aspect of personal liberty is fundamental?"[4]

The 7-2 *Roe* decision held that "the Constitution protects a fundamental 'right of privacy,' broad enough to encompass a woman's decision whether or not to terminate her pregnancy."[5] The Court ruled that the 14th Amendment, which protects individual liberty, guarantees an adult woman the right to seek a termination of her pregnancy until viability, when the unborn child could live outside its mother's womb.

Like many Supreme Court rulings, however, *Roe v. Wade* left many issues unaddressed: Can a minor have an abortion without her parents' consent or notification? Does the federal government have to subsidize abortions for low-income women? Can the state regulate the safety of the procedure, and if so, to what extent? Many of these issues have been, or will be, resolved in other Supreme Court cases.[6]

Immediately after *Roe v. Wade*, abortion opponents fought to have the ruling overturned. They believed that "the Court had stretched beyond its limits." With the election of Ronald Reagan in 1980, these pro-life advocates had a powerful ally in the office of the president. "Make no mistake," Reagan said, "abortion-on-demand is not a right granted by the Constitution."[7]

Perhaps the biggest flaws in *Roe v. Wade* have emerged due to advances in medical technology. These advances reveal how vague the language of the Court's decision is. For example, the Supreme Court did not address the distinction between terminating pregnancy and terminating the life of a fetus. This distinction could become necessary if, as

During his presidency (1981-1989), Ronald Reagan opposed a woman's right to have an abortion.

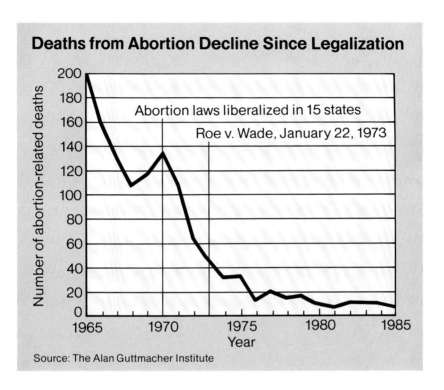

Deaths from Abortion Decline Since Legalization

Abortion laws liberalized in 15 states

Roe v. Wade, January 22, 1973

Number of abortion-related deaths

Year

Source: The Alan Guttmacher Institute

predicted, it becomes possible someday to take a fetus out of its mother's womb before it is viable and somehow provide an artificial womb or transplant it into the womb of a woman who cannot conceive.[8]

Another problem with the Court's ruling involves the issue of viability. *Roe v. Wade* allows states to prohibit abortion once the fetus is viable. But, since 1973, more and more premature babies are surviving outside the womb. Although many scientists are skeptical, others believe that viability will continue to be pushed earlier and earlier. Because of this and other technological reasons, Justice Sandra Day O'Connor wrote in her dissent of another, later abortion case that "*Roe v. Wade* was on a collision course with itself."[9]

After blocking the entry to an abortion clinic, a Catholic nun is being arrested and forcibly removed from the premises.

LEGAL BATTLEGROUND

Roe v. Wade granted women in the United States the right to choose abortion. From 1973 until 1989, the ruling remained firm. However, in 1989, with *Webster v. Reproductive Health Services*, a crack appeared in the foundation of the 1973 landmark decision. By this time, many of the justices who had decided the 1973 *Roe* case had retired. The new Court had a conservative majority, three of whom had been appointed by President Ronald Reagan. As part of the *Webster* ruling, the Court upheld the constitutionality of a Missouri law that sharply restricted the availability of abortion services. It ruled that states may outlaw abortions in public hospitals and clinics and prohibit public employees from assisting in abortions. The Court also ruled that states may require doctors to test the viability of a fetus before performing an abortion on a woman who has been pregnant for 20 or more weeks. The language of the *Webster* ruling also encouraged state legislatures to pass new laws that would limit access to abortion.[1]

The Supreme Court accepted several subsequent abortion cases pertaining mainly to parental consent, federal funding of abortion clinics, and standards and rules such clinics are required to obey. Many pro-choice supporters think that such laws make finding and affording an abortion provider extremely difficult, especially for poor women. Thus abortion, while still legal, is available to fewer people.

To many experts, the future seems clear. As a Planned Parenthood executive stated it, "The post-*Webster* world will look more and more like the one that existed pre-*Roe*. Where a woman lives, how much she earns, and what she knows will determine whether she can obtain a safe, legal abortion."[2]

Much of the continuing legal controversy involves the so-called hard cases—rape and incest. During his first years as president, George Bush said that abortion should be legal for victims of rape or incest, but that he was against the federal government paying for those abortions. What, then, happens to the victims of rape or incest who cannot afford an abortion? In addition to the financial burden, several laws supported by the pro-life movement impose on victims of rape and incest reporting requirements that are nearly impossible to meet. In Idaho, for example, pro-life advocates supported a law that prohibited abortions in pregnancies resulting from rape unless the crime had been reported to the police within seven days. In cases of date rape particularly, young women often hesitate to report the crime. Furthermore, a victim would not know whether the rape resulted in pregnancy within the seven-day time requirement. Measures such as these reduce the number of abortions obtained by women who want abortions and could legally get them.

Less than 1 percent of all the abortions performed in the United States are in cases of rape and incest (See graph on page 11.), but some pro-lifers are still determined to fight each case. Illinois Congressman Henry Hyde sums up the pro-life position: "Rape and incest are tragedies, but why visit on the second victim—the unborn child...capital punishment?"[3] Dr. John Wilke, a leader of one pro-life organization, the National Right to Life Committee, has expressed a more extreme view on the matter of abortion in rape cases: "I don't think we should punish the criminal (a rapist) by killing his child."[4]

Another prime area of dispute involves pregnant teenagers. Becky Bell was in 11th grade when she fell in love with a young man in college. He told her he was **sterile,** so they began having unprotected sex. When she discovered she was pregnant, the man told her to get lost.

After deciding to have an abortion, Becky went to Planned Parenthood, a national organization that provides information on family planning and abortion. At the clinic, she learned that her home state of Indiana requires minors to have the written permission of parents for an abortion. The law allows a judge to waive parental consent in some cases, but that is unusual. Although Becky had a stable family life and a reasonably good relationship with her parents, she told friends that she couldn't tell her parents about being pregnant. "They would be disappointed in me," she explained.

Within a few days, just before turning 17 years old, Becky Bell died. An infection that resulted from a botched, illegal abortion killed her. This tragedy did not occur in the 1950s or 1960s when horror stories of illegal abortions were common. It happened in 1988.

Although keeping the circumstances of Becky's death a secret would have been easier than speaking out, Becky's

Bill and Karen Bell prepare to testify against parental consent laws in Kansas. Their daughter, Becky, (inset) *died after undergoing an illegal abortion.*

parents decided to tell her story. They have become pro-choice activists and often face harsh criticism. Their competence as parents has often been called into question by supporters of the parental consent laws who feel that Becky's pregnancy and subsequent death couldn't have happened to a teenager in a "good" family. An editorial in their hometown newspaper denies the need to change Indiana law, theorizing that Becky caused her own death by experimenting with drugs and sex.

"Campaigning against [parental consent] laws is all we can do now," says Becky's father. "But if I could go back in time, I'd tell Becky she could come to us with any trouble, no matter what."[5]

More than 30 states currently require girls under 18 to notify, or in most cases, to get *permission* from a parent for an abortion. In some states, *both* parents must be notified, even when one parent has not been involved in raising the girl. Permission is required even in cases in which there is evidence of past abuse by the parent. This situation horrifies pro-choice advocates. Tragic results from the parental consent requirement have already occurred. A teenager in Idaho, for example, was murdered by her father in August 1989 after asking his permission to get an abortion.[6]

Public polls indicate that a majority of Americans think parents should be notified of a daughter's intent to get an abortion. Even pro-choice advocates find this a difficult area, because making arguments against parental involvement and communication (even if forced) sounds anti-family. Some argue that since other, much more minor surgical procedures require parental consent, why not abortion?

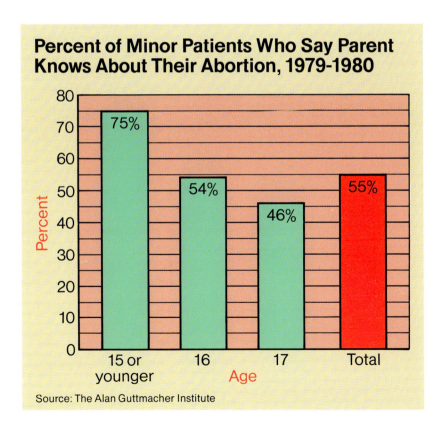

Percent of Minor Patients Who Say Parent Knows About Their Abortion, 1979-1980

Source: The Alan Guttmacher Institute

But the problem of teenage pregnancy is overwhelming. According to surveys, at least half the young people between the ages of 15 and 19 are sexually active, and 24 percent of all teenage girls will become pregnant by age 18.[7] Many of these girls will want an abortion and be faced with parental notification requirements, but communication between parents and children about sexual matters is often extremely difficult. Eventually, of course, the pregnancy will be obvious and the parents will know about it. But meanwhile a teenage girl may put off dealing with her condition, thinking or wishing it would somehow go away by itself. The delay could mean that abortion is no longer a safe, legal option for her.

What effect do parental consent laws have on the number of abortions obtained? Some evidence shows that the impact of such laws is minor. Most girls who normally turn to their parents when in trouble will do so if they become pregnant. But statistics in such states as Minnesota and Massachusetts before and after their parental-involvement laws were enacted show a marked drop in the number of abortions obtained by teenagers after the laws were in place.[8]

One of the most hotly debated Supreme Court rulings—the so-called gag rule—came in May 1991. By a 5-4 majority, the court upheld federal regulations that prohibit employees of federally funded family planning clinics (clinics supported in part by federal taxes) to discuss abortion with their clients. The 4,500 clinics serving nearly 4 million women each year are now required to refer pregnant women for prenatal care and to refuse to help women find doctors who will perform abortions. If asked directly about abortion, staff workers must answer that they "do not consider abortion an appropriate method of family planning."

In 1992 the Bush administration revised the regulation to allow doctors, but no other members of a clinic's staff, to mention abortion. But most people working at clinics and counseling patients are not doctors. In effect, the new version of the gag rule differs little from the original in its impact on clinic activity.

Many clinics stated their intention to continue providing abortion information even though they would lose all federal financing by doing so. Small clinics with few other means of support will probably be unable to afford to take such a stand and will have to close their doors. Many women may find that there are no longer any clinics near them that provide abortions. Travel expenses will have to be added to the cost of the procedure itself.

After the May 1991 decision, the U.S. Congress immediately set in motion two bills intended to overturn the Court's decision. Abortion-rights groups began preparing for a difficult battle. Although pro-choice groups appeared at the time to have a majority of Congress on their side, they were not sure whether the majority would be large enough to override President Bush's inevitable veto of such legislation.[9]

During the early 1990s, many state legislatures passed new laws restricting abortion. The state of Pennsylvania, for example, passed a law called the Abortion Control Act, which regulated access to abortion and challenged *Roe v. Wade* in the Supreme Court in June 1992. The Court ruled that four sections of the Pennsylvania law did not impose an "undue burden" on a woman seeking an abortion. The Court defined undue burden as a "substantial obstacle in the path of a woman seeking an abortion before the fetus attains viability." The Court ruled that four sections of the Pennsylvania law did not impose an undue burden on the right to

How States Line Up on Key Abortion Restrictions

- 🟩 Parental-notification laws
- 🟠 Minors can bypass parental notification with a court order
- ⭐ Waiting period, typically 24 hours
- ✔ Mandatory counseling about fetal development and abortion alternatives

State	🟩	🟠	⭐	✔	State	🟩	🟠	⭐	✔
Alabama	🟩	🟠		✔	Montana	🟩			✔
Alaska	🟩			✔	Nebraska	🟩	🟠		✔
Arizona	🟩	🟠			Nevada	🟩	🟠		✔
Arkansas	🟩	🟠			New Hampshire				
California	🟩	🟠			New Jersey				
Colorado	🟩				New Mexico	🟩			
Connecticut					New York				
Delaware	🟩		⭐	✔	North Carolina				
Florida	🟩	🟠		✔	North Dakota	🟩	🟠	⭐	✔
Georgia	🟩	🟠			Ohio	🟩	🟠	⭐	✔
Hawaii					Oklahoma				
Idaho	🟩		⭐	✔	Oregon				
Illinois	🟩	🟠			Pennsylvania	🟩	🟠	⭐	✔
Indiana	🟩	🟠	⭐	✔	Rhode Island	🟩	🟠		✔
Iowa					South Carolina	🟩	🟠		
Kansas	🟩	🟠	⭐	✔	South Dakota	🟩		⭐	✔
Kentucky	🟩	🟠	⭐	✔	Tennessee	🟩		⭐	✔
Louisiana	🟩	🟠		✔	Texas				
Maine			⭐	✔	Utah	🟩			✔
Maryland	🟩			✔	Vermont				
Massachusetts	🟩	🟠	⭐	✔	Virginia				✔
Michigan	🟩	🟠			Washington				
Minnesota	🟩	🟠			West Virginia	🟩	🟠		
Mississippi	🟩	🟠	⭐	✔	Wisconsin	🟩	🟠		✔
Missouri	🟩	🟠		✔	Wyoming	🟩	🟠		

Sources: National Abortion Rights Action League; The Alan Guttmacher Institute

How States Rank on Access to Legal Abortions

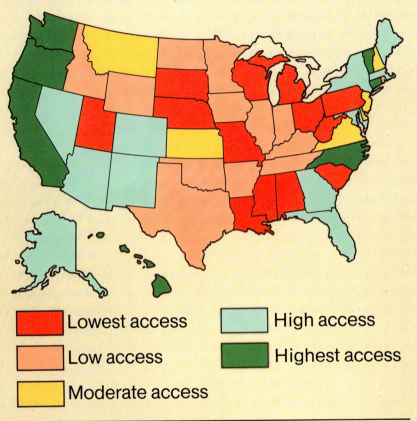

🟥 Lowest access	🟦 High access
🟧 Low access	🟩 Highest access
🟨 Moderate access	

Note: Rankings were based on evaluation of responses to the following:

- Does the governor support legal abortion?
- Does the legislature support legal abortion?
- Does the state enforce restrictions?
- Has the state enacted new restrictions?
- Does the state provide legal protection for abortion?

Source: National Abortion Rights Action League

In 1992 the Supreme Court (top) heard Planned Parenthood v. Casey. Attorney Kathryn Kolbert (bottom, left), who represented the abortion-rights side in the case, and Pennsylvania Attorney General Ernest D. Preate, Jr., (bottom, far right) addressed the media after appearing before the Court.

abortion and were therefore constitutional. These sections require a woman to delay an abortion for 24 hours after visiting a medical office and listening to a presentation designed to change her decision to abort; to require teenagers to have the consent of one parent or a judge; to specify the medical emergencies in which the other requirements will be waived; and to require a doctor or clinic to make statistical reports to the state. However, by a 5-4 vote, the Court struck down a fifth provision requiring a married woman to tell her husband of her intent to have an abortion. Although the Pennsylvania decision limited access to abortion, it explicitly upheld a woman's legal right to abortion. The 1992 Supreme Court decision also prompted many members of Congress to step up efforts to pass a federal law protecting a woman's right to legal abortion.

Is abortion a legal question only in the United States? No, abortion law is an issue in several other countries. For example, during the reign of the infamous, recently executed dictator Nicolae Ceauşescu, Romanian women were closely watched, even examined regularly, to make sure they did not practice birth control or obtain abortions. Ceauşescu was determined to increase Romania's population dramatically. Women who wanted to control their fertility by practicing birth control were treated as criminals.

The situation in Romania during Ceauşescu's decades of ironfisted rule, however, was unusual. No clear link exists between political freedom and a pro-choice position on abortion. In fact, it appears that the countries with the most abortions are also among the most politically repressive.[10]

The former Soviet Union and the countries of Eastern Europe legalized abortion many years before the United States did so. The issue in those countries was not women's rights versus fetal rights, however. The problem was overpopulation. Contraceptives were, and still are, largely unavailable in those countries. Consequently, one in five women living in the former Soviet Union has an abortion each year. This amounts to somewhere between 8 and 16 million abortions annually.[11]

In recent years, some countries have gone even further in a desperate effort to control population. The official policy in China allows a couple to have only one child. Because China has gone through a period of population growth that threatens social goals and the quality of life, birth control is of utmost importance. Chinese policymakers have agreed to force pregnant women who already have one child to have mandatory abortions if they become pregnant again.[12]

According to the figures of the Alan Guttmacher Institute, almost 40 percent of the world's population lives in countries where abortion is available on request. An additional 24 percent live in countries (like the United States, most Western European nations, Japan, and Australia) where women can get abortions for a wide array of medical, economic, or social reasons.[13]

Pro-life movements have sprouted in many areas of the world besides the United States. Ambivalence about abortion can be seen perhaps most symbolically in Japan, where abortion has been legal since the 1940s. Japanese Buddhism acknowledges the pain felt over the baby who might have been born and recognizes abortion as a deeply disturbing part of some women's lives. In Japan special statues or shrines are erected at which women can mourn the deaths of their unborn children. Resembling abstract human forms without specific features, rows and rows of these small monuments stand like gravestones in a cemetery.[14]

A Chinese child stands under a poster urging couples to have no more than one child.

These Romanian orphans seem lost in a long line of cribs. In Bucharest many such homes are filled with orphans hoping for adoptive parents.

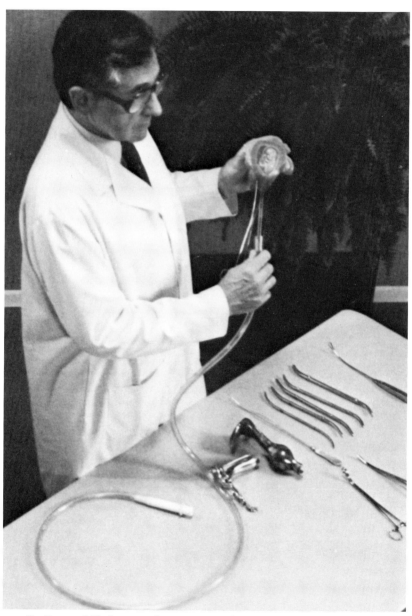

Dr. Bernard Nathanson demonstrates the vacuum-aspiration abortion procedure, which takes four to seven minutes to perform.

METHODS
OF ABORTION

Abortion dates back to the beginning of civilization. Many methods used by women and by doctors—such as inserting pastes made of mashed ants and gunpowder into the uterus, or assaulting the belly with boiling water or stones—were extremely painful. Obviously, many methods used in the past failed to work and caused damage or even death to the woman.[1]

Legal abortions are now viewed as medically safe and simple. Teenagers, for example, are 24 times more likely to die from childbirth than from a first-trimester abortion.[2] It is 352 times safer to have an abortion than to have an appendix removed.[3] Of course, all medical procedures, including abortions, involve some risk. With abortion, the risks of complications, such as infections and injuries to the **cervix** or uterus, increase with the length of the pregnancy.

While legal abortions are considered medically safe, *illegal* abortions are usually considered far more dangerous. The following statistics provide some proof of this: Approximately the same number of abortions are performed in Mexico as in the United States. In the United States, where abortion is currently legal, an average of six abortions per year result in the mother's death; in Mexico, where abortion is illegal, approximately 140,000 women die each year.[4]

The safest time for an abortion is between 7 and 12 weeks of pregnancy, when the fetus is no larger than a lima bean or a walnut and is not fully formed. The type of procedure done at this point is called a vacuum-aspiration or suction abortion, which takes four to seven minutes to perform. Over 90 percent of all abortions are done in this way.[5]

Between the 12th and 16th week, one of two other procedures is usually used. Both require general anesthesia and are more costly and uncomfortable than the vacuum-aspiration method. During the more common procedure **dilation and curettage** (D & C), the doctor may take 12 to 20 minutes to dilate the cervix (that is, to widen the opening to the uterus) and scrape and suction out the contents of the uterus.[6] The **dilation and evacuation** (D & E) method involves crushing the fetus and then extracting it with forceps. Many doctors refuse to perform D & E operations.[7]

If the pregnancy has progressed beyond 16 weeks, a doctor injects a saline solution into the woman's body to start labor contractions, which, in turn, cause the uterus to push out the fetus. This procedure, which must be done in a hospital, is far more costly and painful than a vacuum-aspiration abortion. In addition, the woman usually has to stay in the hospital two to three days.[8]

Whenever possible, doctors try to avoid performing abortions after the first trimester (beyond 13 weeks). But sometimes a frightened woman, especially someone very young, will deny what is happening to her body, or try to wish it away until it's too late to perform the simple abortion procedure.

Another common reason for abortions after the first few months of pregnancy is that doctors have detected abnormalities in the fetus. The medical procedure known as **amniocentesis**–withdrawing some of the fluid surrounding the fetus so it can be analyzed–cannot be done until the woman is at least 13 weeks pregnant, and the results take an additional two to six weeks. But only a small proportion of abortions (between 1 in 1,000 and 30 in 1,000) are performed for reasons of fetal abnormality.[9]

The decision to abort because of fetal abnormality is a difficult one and raises many ethical questions. Does a

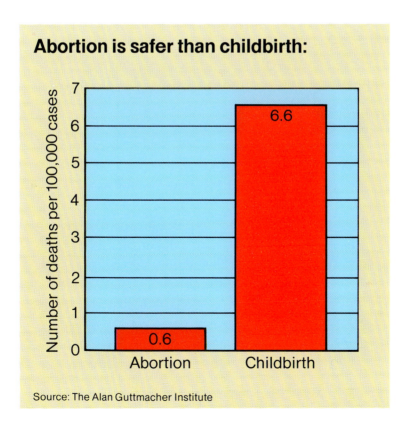

Abortion is safer than childbirth:

Source: The Alan Guttmacher Institute

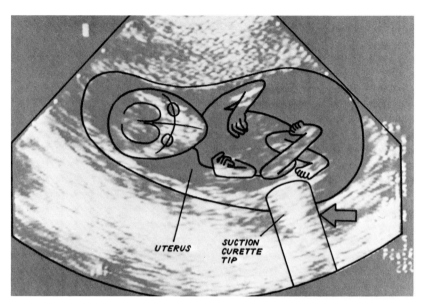

In a scene from The Silent Scream, *Dr. Bernard Nathanson demonstrates the position of the fetus in the ultrasound image on the screen. The drawing at the top shows the insertion of the suction curette tip into the uterus during a vacuum-aspiration abortion.*

woman choose abortion to prevent a child's being born only to suffer intense pain before its early death? Or, do some women choose abortion because caring for an abnormal child would be inconvenient, perhaps even a hardship on the mother? What about cases in which the child would be expected to live, but only with a diminished "quality" of life. Who is in a position to determine *what* quality level makes life worth living and what does not? Because of these and other ethical questions, many women allow their pregnancies to continue even after doctors have detected abnormality.

After 24 weeks of pregnancy, the fetus is considered viable and an abortion will not be performed. If there is a medical emergency, a live birth will probably be attempted, and the hospital staff will fight to keep the premature baby alive.

Two other abortion methods should be mentioned here. One is not widely discussed, but is used in many hospitals in cases of rape. The "morning-after" pill combines certain dosages of female hormones and, when taken within 72 hours of unprotected intercourse, will usually prevent a fertilized egg from implanting in the uterus.[10] This procedure is considered preventative, and no one ever knows whether the sexual contact would have resulted in pregnancy.

For an already traumatized rape victim, being given the morning-after pill is much easier than facing a possible abortion later. But some hospitals and clinics dealing with rape victims do not always mention the possibility of its use. Why? Many pro-life advocates oppose the use of the morning-after pill under any circumstances. In addition, any large dose of hormones carries a risk, and some experts question this pill's effect on the future pregnancies of women who have taken it.

Even more controversial than the morning-after pill is RU-486, the so-called French abortion pill. Developed in the late 1980s, RU-486 has been shown to be a safe and effective method of inducing early abortion about 96 percent of the time. Widely used in France and China, this abortion pill is also considered a promising treatment for several serious illnesses, such as cancer, osteoporosis, and diabetes.[11]

As soon as the French manufacturer, Roussel Uclaf, introduced RU-486, however, American pro-life groups moved to prevent distribution of the drug in the United States. They threatened protests against the French manufacturer and indicated they would boycott its products as well as those of related companies in other European countries and in the United States.

In 1991, however, the New Hampshire legislature invited Roussel to test the drug in its state. The New Hampshire tests of RU-486 began the process of getting it approved by the Food and Drug Administration (FDA), which must test and approve all drugs before they can be made available to the American public. Other states are considering similar measures, and many people think that in time RU-486 will be available in the United States.[12]

Pro-life advocates say that the use of this drug is murder just as much as surgical abortion is. Moreover, they warn that taking RU-486 is not as simple as it sounds. The abortion pill requires trained medical guidance and the simultaneous use of other substances. And what if the drug fails? If the women who take RU-486 do not then get surgical abortions, many pro-lifers fear the result might be an epidemic of deformed babies.

When a woman thinking of having an abortion seeks counseling and information, she may find two very different types of family planning clinics. Some clinics that advertise free pregnancy testing are strongly anti-abortion. They often show the pregnant woman a graphic film of a second trimester abortion to persuade her against aborting the fetus. For some women, this experience is frightening and confusing. But for others who are feeling forced into an abortion by a man, by society, or by other factors, this type of clinic can arm her with arguments against abortion.

The other type of family planning clinic usually provides counseling about the methods of abortion, about alternatives to abortion, and about the emotional issues involved. In most of these clinics, the intent is to help a woman make an informed decision. If a clinic staff leans strongly in favor of choosing abortion, however, it is not likely to provide much counseling about keeping a baby and trying to raise it.[13]

The Planned Parenthood Federation of America is perhaps the best known network of family planning clinics in the United States. Although its name has become closely identified with abortion, Planned Parenthood emphasizes its commitment to provide reproductive health services—family planning, counseling, and various educational and other health-related services–to women. Margaret Sanger founded Planned Parenthood in 1916 to promote the use of contraception, and the privately funded group has grown steadily ever since. Planned Parenthood's 850 clinics serve nearly 4 million clients each year.[14]

Planned Parenthood is the prime target for pro-life activists. Randall Terry of Operation Rescue considers it "the single largest child killer in the U.S." But this characterization is misleading. In 1988, for instance, Planned Parenthood accounted for only 104,000 of the 1.6 million abortions performed in the United States.[15]

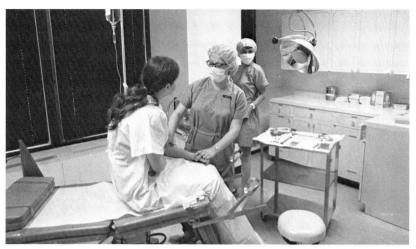

Nurses prepare a patient for an abortion in a New York clinic.

If it's not the number of abortions that make this organization such an enemy of pro-life activists, its aggressive tactics and political success may be contributing factors. Recently, Planned Parenthood has become embroiled in Supreme Court decisions, and it represents, for many pro-choice advocates, the strongest hope of maintaining abortion rights. After the Supreme Court ruling that federally funded clinics could not discuss abortion with their patients, Planned Parenthood announced that it would do without $30 million of federal funding rather than restrict its counseling in this way. Many other clinics, however, will not be able to survive without government money.

Some experts believe that the legal status of abortion is becoming less important than its decreasing availability. Even before the gag rule, more than 82 percent of the counties in the United States (especially in rural areas) were without any abortion providers at all.[16] Pro-choice advocates point out that the availability of abortion has steadily declined with each Supreme Court decision since *Webster.* This is especially true for women who have depended on public facilities and aid—the women who can least afford children.

Furthermore, fewer and fewer doctors are willing to learn or to perform abortion procedures because they fear being targeted by pro-life radicals. If clinics and doctors are not providing abortions, the number of safe, legal abortions performed will diminish regardless of the fate of *Roe v. Wade.*

Many pro-choice groups are preparing for a future without *Roe* and without legal abortion in many states. Activists are discussing ways to organize an "abortion underground," a network to help women get to states where abortion is available. Others urge a more radical solution—women themselves learning to perform an abortion procedure called **menstrual extraction,** a technique that is similar to vacuum aspiration.

Women without medical training can be taught to do this procedure safely and inexpensively at home, but medical expertise is always necessary, and should be easily available if something goes wrong. If menstrual extraction is attempted more than six weeks after a woman's last period, severe complications are likely.[17]

The very fact that such radical ideas as home abortion are being discussed indicates that women will get abortions one way or another. Before *Roe*, as many as 1.2 million women obtained illegal abortions each year.[18]

Pro-life advocates are saddened by such an outlook. They insist that there must be a better way than abortion. Are pro-life advocates unrealistic to expect that abortions will end if they are illegal and difficult to obtain? Or do they simply see an ideal world worth striving for?

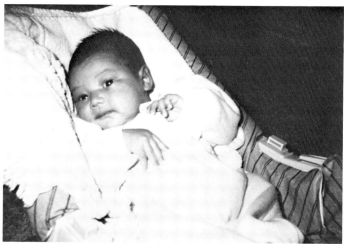

Counselors in centers run by pro-life advocates meet with women in crisis pregnancy situations (top). Many of these women choose adoption for their babies over abortion. This baby (bottom) is just one example.

ALTERNATIVES
TO ABORTION

Karen was 20 years old when she gave up her newborn daughter for adoption. An unmarried college student, she was convinced she was doing the right thing for the child. But the existence of that girl, somewhere out in the world, has haunted Karen ever since. Every year, she celebrates her daughter's birthday, but it is not a joyful celebration. Karen says that someday, if possible, she will find her daughter, explain things to her, maybe even apologize, and tell her she loves her.

Another young mother, Molly, gave up her baby for adoption, and says, "I miss her *so* much. I always feel like there's a piece of something missing in my life . . . I see an ad for a diaper commerical. And it hits me . . . but you know, then I think about the good family she's in. And I feel better. But it still gets me." [1]

Both of these young women made painful decisions, but both believe they did the right thing, as do thousands like them.

Each year more than one million American teenage girls between the ages of 15 and 19 become pregnant. An additional 30,000 pregnancies occur among girls under the age of 15.[2] About 400,000 of these pregnant teens currently get abortions, accounting for roughly one-fourth of the approximately 1.6 million abortions performed each year.

"We must change from abortion to adoption," says President George Bush. Many people look to adoption as the most positive solution to an unplanned pregnancy. Married couples who are unable to conceive children and young, pregnant women would seem the perfect match. As stated by an attorney who handles adoption cases, "The baby gets the family that [the birth mother] can't give it. She gets her baby rescued, her future restored, her life back in her own hands. The couple that can't have a baby gets the baby they've always been dreaming of. There are no losers in this transaction."[3]

But the rallying cry "adoption, not abortion" angers many experts. "We shouldn't be looking for magic answers to complex problems," says Frank Bonati, president of a Pittsburgh adoption agency. "Couples looking to adopt children and women with unwanted pregnancies face agonizing decisions. Superficial slogans don't help."[4] Karen and Molly would probably agree.

If abortion becomes illegal and more women give birth rather than abort, adoption agencies may be unable to handle all the additional cases while still thoroughly checking prospective parents. An increase in the number of "baby brokers"—people who basically buy and sell babies—could result as well. They could easily take financial advantage of desperate people on both sides of the adoption equation.

In addition to these concerns, many doctors say that encouraging young girls to go through the full pregnancy,

Miami's Jackson Memorial Hospital has been the only home to this child, who is shown here on his second birthday. His mother died of AIDS and his father has the disease, so this child has little chance of being adopted.

labor, and delivery, even if they plan to give the babies up for adoption, is irresponsible. For teenagers, especially those 15 and under, giving birth carries a high risk of complications for both the mother and the baby. In fact, pregnancy has been found to be far more dangerous than early abortion.

What if abortion became illegal or otherwise unavailable to most of the 400,000 teenagers who currently get abortions each year? There might be adoptive homes for all the healthy white infants, but children with disabilities and those of other races might lose out. According to recent statistics, "black women account for close to 30 percent of all abortions, although blacks only make up 12 percent of the population. Experts estimate that 40 percent of all children now up for

Adoption agencies like to match prospective parents with children of the same race and ethnic background.

adoption are black, and few agencies will cross racial lines when matching babies with prospective parents."[5] In other words, adoption agencies want to match black children with black adoptive parents, Asian with Asian, Hispanic with Hispanic, and so on. Handicapped children are also likely to wait years for families, and many will never find them.

Another major problem with adoption involves the alarming number of "crack babies" and other children who are disadvantaged because of poor prenatal care. Those who survive the first few years have severe problems that do not end in infancy. At least 375,000 babies are born each year to mothers who use drugs, a number that tripled between 1985 and 1990. Too few foster homes and adoptive parents are available for these children. Moreover, AIDS among newborns who got the virus from their mothers will almost certainly become more widespread. Will foster homes and adoptive parents be available for these children?[6]

Planned Parenthood clinics offer various methods of birth control. Here, a client is learning the proper use of a condom, one of many options.

Many teenage mothers choose to keep their babies.

Pro-choice advocates emphasize the difficulties involved with adoption, especially the physical and emotional trauma experienced by many women who give birth and then give up their babies. And to many people, it seems particularly cruel to expect a rape victim to go through with a pregnancy resulting from that crime. But even in this worst-case scenario, is abortion always the best solution?

Lee Ezell says no. Thirty years ago she was a 14-year-old rape victim who now says she's grateful that an easy abortion was not available to her. "Abortion," she says, "is too permanent an answer for a temporary problem. Abortion is not an answer, it is an additional problem to be reckoned with later...[and] will not solve the problem of victimization."[7]

Ezell gave up her baby for adoption at birth and never had another child. Years later, however, she got a phone call from her daughter, Julie, who had been searching for her. She wanted to let her mother know that she'd just had a baby herself, and she wanted to express her gratitude to the woman who had, in spite of tragic circumstances, chosen to give her life.[8] The happy ending to this story supports the pro-life belief that everything will work out if a pregnancy is allowed to continue to birth.

Alternatives to adoption and abortion also exist. At least 93 percent of pregnant teens decide to keep their babies and do not seek abortion or adoption. Being an "unwed mother" doesn't appear to carry the same stigma it did a generation ago. In fact, with celebrities boasting of their single-parent status, having a baby to raise alone may look "cool" to some girls. They usually receive some form of government aid, or they get help from parents or other family members, or, more rarely, they marry or live with the father of the child.[9]

These poor, homeless women and children wait outside the Lincoln Motel in Newark, New Jersey, to see whether the state will pay for their housing. The special fund that allowed homeless families to stay in motels had run out.

Reality may hit hard, however. Eight out of 10 girls who have babies at 17 or younger drop out of high school.[10] Divorce is much more likely in teen marriages "forced" by pregnancy, and many parents of teen mothers are unable—financially, emotionally, or in other ways—to help. The baby, therefore, may be raised by poor, undereducated, young women with few parenting skills and virtually no hope.

Various research studies show that many women who are denied abortions carry around resentment and anger toward their children for years. The results may be more disastrous than previously realized. Children born to these women appear to have a tendency toward health problems, trouble in school, and trouble with the law.

Doctors, psychologists, and social workers frequently see babies and children who have "failed to thrive" due to depressed, inattentive parents. They see mothers who behave mechanically or angrily toward their "burdens," prop bottles in their children's mouths rather than cuddling them during feeding, fail to give crucial verbal stimulation, and leave babies in cribs so long that they develop bald spots on the backs of their heads.[11]

Of course, not all non-nurturing parents have considered or been denied abortion. Parenting skills are not acquired naturally. Like language and other social skills, they are learned, primarily by example. A young mother who herself was reared in poverty, perhaps even abused or neglected, may be the only nurturing adult in her own baby's life. That baby becomes part of a tragic chain of events and is likely to continue the same pattern, having babies young, alone, and in poverty.

Meghan, a sophomore at a large urban high school in the midwest, says, "I see girls my age with unwanted babies all the time. Our school has a big nursery set up for them. When I talk to them, most of them say the babies ruined their lives, and I wonder how that makes them treat those babies. I saw one girl coming to school with a three-week-old with no hat or mittens or booties on the baby even though it was like a -20° below windchill outside. A few months later, I saw she was pregnant again. I asked her if she had considered abortion this time, and she said, 'No. I'm pro-life.' I don't understand that at all."

One New York prison has a parenting class for its female inmates. According to one of the staff members, on one typical day, a young inmate entered who was pregnant with her 14th child. She had the first when she was 10 years old, the result of a rape. Her father does not believe in abortion. Among three other young inmates, they have 18 children in foster care. The teacher asked one of the women her new child's name, but she couldn't remember it. "I just call her 'Kiddo,' " she said.[12]

The one thing most people agree on is that abortions should be prevented. *How* is the problem. From the pro-life viewpoint, teaching children to abstain from premarital sex is the most important factor. Many pro-life supporters oppose sex education in the schools because they believe teaching birth control or methods for "safe sex" encourages premarital sex, even promiscuity. Many married couples who are pro-life oppose birth control as well as abortion. They believe that nature alone should determine the number of babies a married couple has.

Pro-choice advocates strongly favor sex education as long as it also teaches responsibility in sexual behavior. They also push for further research on birth control methods, research some pro-life supporters have effectively blocked by threatening to boycott drug companies engaged in it. According to the National Research Council, as many as three million unwanted pregnancies occur each year because of contraceptive failure. It is possible that one-third to one-half of all abortions could be prevented by more and better birth-control options.[13]

SEEKING A COMMON GROUND

The scene is all too familiar—angry mobs shouting at each other across barricades; placards with pictures of bloody fetuses on one side, placards with pictures of bloody coat hangers on the other. Such scenes oversimplify the abortion issue.

In reality, most people have deep, ambivalent feelings about abortion. One person might comment, "Yes, it's necessary sometimes, but no, not always." Or, "I could never have one, but I think others should have the choice." Or, "My religious beliefs are important to me, and they tell me that it's wrong, period. Except . . . ."

We might like the issue to go away because we are all weary of it. Unfortunately, the argument will probably rage on with little hope of resolution until we can find some common ground. When that happens, perhaps the boundless energy of protesters on both sides of the abortion issue can be channeled into other areas of concern for children—born and unborn.

Resources to Contact

Alan Guttmacher Institute
111 Fifth Avenue
New York, NY 10003
212-254-5656

American Life League, Inc.
P.O. Box 1350
Stafford, VA 22554
703-659-4171

Americans United for Life
343 South Dearborn Street
Suite 1804
Chicago, IL 60604
312-786-9494

Catholics for a Free Choice
1436 U Street, N.W.
Suite 301
Washington, D.C. 20009
202-986-6093

The Center for Population Options
1025 Vermont Avenue, N.W.
Suite 210
Washington, D.C. 20005
202-347-5700

Christian Action Council
101 West Broad Street
Suite 500
Falls Church, VA 22046
703-237-2100

Eagle Forum
P.O. Box 618
Alton, IL 62002
(No telephone number listed)

Feminist Majority Foundation
P.O. Box 96780
Washington, D.C. 20077
703-522-2214

Feminists for Life of America
811 East Forty-seventh Street
Kansas City, MO 64110
816-753-2130

National Abortion Federation
1436 U Street, N.W.
Suite 103
Washington, D.C. 20009
202-667-5881 or
1-800-772-9100

National Abortion Rights
Action League
1101 Fourteenth Street
Washington, D.C. 20005
202-408-4600

National Organization for Women
1000 Sixteenth Street, N.W.
Washington, D.C. 20036
202-331-0066

National Right to Life Committee
419 Seventh Street, N.W.
Station 500
Washington, D.C. 20004
202-626-8800

Operation Rescue
P.O. Box 1180
Binghamton, NY 13902
607-723-4012

Planned Parenthood Federation
  of America, Inc.
810 Seventh Avenue
New York, NY 10019
212-541-7800 or
1-800-473-7732
(Consult your telephone
directory for an office near you.)

Pro-Choice Resources
3255 Hennepin Avenue South
Suite 227
Minneapolis, MN 55408
612-825-9122

Pro-Life Action League
6160 North Cicero Avenue
Chicago, IL 60646
312-777-2900

Religious Coalition for
  Abortion Rights
100 Maryland Avenue, N.E.
Washington, D.C. 20002
202-543-0224

U.S. House of Representatives
The Honorable Congressman
  or Congresswoman _____
Washington, D.C. 20515
202-224-3121

U.S. Senate
The Honorable Senator _____
Washington, D.C. 20510
202-224-3121

White House
President _____
1600 Pennsylvania Avenue, N.W.
Washington, D.C. 20500
202-456-1414 or
202-456-1111

Endnotes

CHAPTER 1. DIFFICULT CHOICES

[1] "The Abortion Decision: Readers Respond," *U.S. News and World Report* (August 7, 1989), 23.

[2] Kristin Luker, *Abortion and the Politics of Motherhood* (Berkeley and Los Angeles: University of California Press, 1984), 2.

[3] Daniel Callahan, "An Ethical Challenge to Pro-choice Advocates," *Commonweal* (November 23, 1990), 683.

[4] Jodi Jacobson, "The Global Politics of Abortion," *Utne Reader* (March/April, 1991), 56.

[5] Callahan, 683.

[6] Richard Lacayo, "Abortion, the Future Is already Here," *Time* (May 4, 1992), 28.

[7] Editors, *Christianity Today* (December 17, 1990), 49.

[8] Lacayo, 28.

[9] Marlene Gerber Fried, Ed., *From Abortion to Reproductive Freedom: Transforming a Movement* (Boston: South End Press, 1990), 129.

[10] Ibid.

[11] Ibid.

[12] Callahan, 684.

[13] Angela Bonavoglia, Ed., *The Choices We Made* (New York: Random House, 1991), 116.

[14] Richard Lacayo, "Whose Life Is It?" *Time,* May 1, 1989, 24.

[15] Sue Nathanson, *Soul Crisis* (New York: New American Library, 1989), 6.

[16] Ibid., 54.

[17] Ibid., 2.

[18] Tim Stafford, "The Abortion Wars," *Christianity Today*, October 6, 1989, 684.

[19] Callahan, 684.

[20] Luker, 10.

CHAPTER 2. WHEN DOES LIFE BEGIN?

[1] Lacayo, "Whose Life Is It?" 21.

[2] Human Life Alliance Newspaper Supplement, Spring 1991, 4.

[3] Charles A. Gardner, "Is An Embryo A Person?" *The Nation*, November 13, 1989, 558.

[4] Carl Sagan and Ann Druyan, "Is It Possible To Be Pro-Life and Pro-Choice?" *Parade Magazine*, April 22, 1990, 6.

[5] Human Life Alliance, 1.

[6] Sagan, 6.

[7] Human Life Alliance, 3.

[8] Sagan, 6.

[9] Human Life Alliance, 3.

[10] Sagan, 6.

[11] Human Life Alliance, 3.

[12] Gardner, 559.

[13] Luker, 5-6.

[14] William Saletan, "If Fetuses Are People..." *The New Republic*, September 18 and 25, 1989, 19.

[15] Gardner, 557.

[16] "Court Rules for Ex-husband in Frozen-embryo Case," Minneapolis *Star Tribune*, June 2, 1992.

[17] Fried, 269-270.

CHAPTER 3. WOMANHOOD AND MOTHERHOOD

[1] Luker, x.

[2] Nathanson, 31, quoting from Esther Harding's *The Way of All Women*.

[3] Nathanson, 219, quoting Kathryn Allen Rabuzzi's *Motherself: A Mythic Analysis of Motherhood*.

[4] Luker, xi.

[5] Bonavoglia, 9.

[6] Fifteen American Women, "Soujourner: The Women's Forum," excerpted in *Utne Reader*, March/April, 1991, 61.

[7] Ibid.

CHAPTER 4. CRUSADERS FOR "LIFE" AND FOR "CHOICE"

[1] Sue Hutchison & James Baker, "The Right-To-Life Shock Troops," *Newsweek*, May 1, 1989, 32.

[2] Ibid.

[3] Ibid.

[4] Fried, 195.

[5] Marian Faux, *Crusaders: Voices from the Abortion Front* (New York: Carol Publishing Group,1990), 136.

[6] Ann Baker, "Prochoice Activism Springs from Many Sources," in Fried, 180.

[7] Dázon Dixon, "Operation Oppress You: Women's Rights Under Siege," in Fried, 185-186.

[8] Tim Stafford, "The Abortion Wars," *Christianity Today*, October 6, 1989, 18.

[9] Luker, 33.

[10] Ibid., 91.

[11] Faux, 5-7.

[12] Eloise Salholz et al., "The Battle Over Abortion," *Newsweek*, May 1, 1989, 31.

[13] Faux, 7.

[14] Ibid., 8.

[15] Richard Lacayo, "The Shouting of the Lambs," *Time*, May 4, 1992, 30.

[16] Faux, 7.

[17] Priscilla Painton, "Buffalo: Operation Fizzle," *Time*, May 4, 1992, 33.

[18] Salholz, 31.

[19] Planned Parenthood pamphlet.

[20] Nancy Amidei, "Variant Views of Abortion," *Commonweal*, October 26, 1990, 597.

[21] Ibid.

[22] Callahan, 683.

[23] Ibid.

[24] Nathanson, 121.

CHAPTER 5. THE MORALITY OF ABORTION

[1] Planned Parenthood pamphlet.

[2] Bonavoglia, 186.

[3] Sagan, 5.

[4] Callahan, 686.

[5] Ibid., 682.

[6] "The Abortion Decision: Readers Respond," *U.S. News and World Report*, August 7, 1989, 23.

[7] Salholz et al., 31.

[8] Callahan, 684.

[9] Kenneth S. Kantzer, "If Both Sides Would Listen," *Christianity Today*, July 14, 1989, 38.

[10] Callahan, 684.

[11] James R. Kelly, "Beyond Slogans: An Abortion Ethic for Women and the Unborn," *The Christian Century*, February 21, 1990, 186, and Rosaline Petchesky, "Giving Women a Real Choice, *The Nation*, May 28, 1990, 734.

[12] Kelly, 185.

[13] Stephen G. Post, "Fetal Tissue Transplant: The Right to Question Progress," *America*, January 12, 1991, 16.

CHAPTER 6. *ROE V. WADE*

[1] Carol A. Emmens, *The Abortion Controversy* (New York: Julian Messner, 1987), 42.

[2] Susan Neiburg Terkel, *Abortion: Facing the Issues* (New York: Franklin Watts, 1988), 13-16.

[3] Archibald Cox, *The Court and the Constitution* (Boston: Houghton Mifflin, 1987), 323.

[4] Ibid., 329.

[5] Ibid.

[6] Terkel, 29.

[7] Ibid., 38.

[8] Ibid., 40.

[9] Ibid.

CHAPTER 7. LEGAL BATTLEGROUND

[1] Ann McDaniel, "The Future of Abortion," *Newsweek*, July 17, 1989, 14.

[2] Eloise Salholz, et. al., "Voting in Curbs and Confusion," *Newsweek*, July 17, 1989, 20.

[3] Margaret Carlson, "Abortion's Hardest Cases," *Time*, July 9, 1990, 25-26.

[4] Planned Parenthood pamphlet.

[5] Ilene Barth, "Abortion Was Seventeen-year-old's Deadly Secret," Minneapolis *Star Tribune*, October 17, 1990.

[6] B. D.Colen, "Mother, May I?" *Health*, October, 1990, 43.

[7] Carlson, 24.

[8] Ibid.

[9] Linda Greenhouse, "Five Justices Uphold U.S. Ruling Curbing Abortion Advice," *The New York Times*, May 14, 1991.

[10] Randy Frame, "Abortion Around the World," *Christianity Today*, February 19, 1990, 30.

[11] Ibid.

[12] Baird & Rosenbaum, 7-8.

[13] Frame, 31-32.

[14] Nathanson, 219, and Frame, 31.

CHAPTER 8. METHODS OF ABORTION

[1] Emmens, 96.

[2] Carlson, 25.

[3] Emmens, 10-11.

[4] Bonavoglia, xxiii.

[5] Emmens, 9.

[6] Carolyn Simpson, *Coping With An Unplanned Pregnancy* (New York: The Rosen Publishing Group, 1990), 16.

[7] Emmens, 9.

[8] Simpson, 16-17.

[9] Emmens, 15.

[10] Bonavoglia, 182.

[11] "Scientists End Study Using 'Abortion Pill,' " *Star Tribune*, reprinted from *The New York Times*, November 16, 1990.

[12] "Bucking the Pro-Lifers," *Time*, May 20, 1991, 50.

[13] Simpson, 16-17.

[14] Marianne Szegedy-Maszak, "Calm, Cool & Beleaguered," *The New York Times Magazine*, August 6, 1989, 18.

[15] Ibid.,19.

[16] Petchesky, Rosalind, "Giving Women a Real Choice," *The Nation*, May 28, 1990, 734.

[17] Layaco, "Abortion, The Future is Already Here," 32.

[18] Ibid.

CHAPTER 9. ALTERNATIVES TO ABORTION

[1] Bob Ehlert, "Molly's Choice," *Star Tribune Sunday Magazine*, December 17, 1989, 13.

[2] Keith Melville, Ed., *The Battle Over Abortion* (Dayton, Ohio: National Issues Forums Institute, 1990), 23.

[3] Ehlert, 13.

[4] Barbara Kantrowitz, "Defying Simple Slogans," *Newsweek*, May 1, 1989, 36.

[5] Ibid.

[6] Barbara Kantrowitz, "The Crack Children," *Newsweek*, February 12, 1990, 62.

[7] Lee Ezell, "She Is Thankful Easy Abortion Wasn't Offered after Her Rape," *St. Paul Pioneer Press*, February 28, 1992.

[8] Ibid.

[9] Kantrowitz, "Defying...," 36.

[10] Carlson, 25.

[11] George F. Will, "Mothers Who Don't Know How," *Newsweek*, April 23, 1990, 80.

[12] Jean Harris, "Abortion: An Inmate's View," *The New York Times*, June 25, 1991.

[13] Salholz, "Politics and the Pill," *Newsweek*, February 26, 1990, 42.

Glossary

abortion: the deliberate termination (ending) of a pregnancy

amniocentesis: a medical procedure that involves the withdrawal of a small amount of fluid from the membranelike sac surrounding the fetus in the uterus. The fluid is used to diagnose possible fetal abnormalities.

cervix: the opening to the uterus

conception: the fertilization of an ovum (mature egg cell) in a woman's body by a sperm cell from a man's body

contraception: the deliberate prevention of conception or pregnancy. Some methods (the pill, diaphragm, and the IUD) require a medical exam. Others (condoms, creams, suppositories, and the sponge) do not and can be purchased at drugstores and pharmacies.

dilation and curettage (D & C): an abortion procedure used between the 12th and 16th weeks of pregnancy. A doctor dilates the cervix (widens the opening to the uterus) and scrapes and suctions out the contents. This procedure requires general anesthesia.

dilation and evacuation (D & E): an abortion procedure occasionally used between the 12th and 16th weeks of pregnancy. A doctor dilates the cervix and then crushes the fetus and extracts it with forceps. This procedure requires general anesthesia.

embryo: the name often used for a fetus between the time of implantation in the uterus and the end of the eighth week after conception

fetal tissue: the remains of a fetus after abortion or miscarriage. Fetal tissue is useful in medical research to treat diseases such as Parkinson's, Alzheimer's, and diabetes.

fetus: an unborn, developing human

menstrual extraction: a home-abortion procedure in which a suction technique similar to the one used in the vacuum aspiration process is used to terminate a pregnancy during the first three months

miscarriage: expulsion of a fetus from the uterus before viability, when it could survive on its own

RU-486: commonly called the French abortion pill. RU-486 must be taken within the first seven weeks of pregnancy with an additional drug that induces contractions. It causes the uterine lining to discharge blood and tissue as during a normal menstrual period, thus expelling the embryo.

sterile: unable to produce offspring

stillborn: dead at birth

uterus: an organ in the female mammal for containing and nourishing offspring during development prior to birth; also called the womb

vacuum aspiration: an abortion procedure usually used during the first 12 weeks of pregnancy. A suction device withdraws the contents of the uterus. This procedure does not require general anesthesia.

viability: the point at which an offspring can survive outside the mother's uterus (currently considered by most medical experts to be at approximately 24 weeks after conception)

Bibliography

Books

Baird, Robert M. & Stuart E. Rosenbaum, Eds. *The Ethics of Pro-Life vs. Pro-Choice.* Buffalo, NY: Prometheus Books, 1989.

Bonavoglia, Angela, Ed. *The Choices We Made.* New York: Random House, 1991.

Emmens, Carol A. *The Abortion Controversy.* New York: Julian Messner, 1987.

Faux, Marian. *Crusaders: Voices from the Abortion Front.* New York: Carol Publishing Group, 1990.

Fried, Marlene Gerber, Ed. *From Abortion to Reproductive Freedom: Transforming a Movement.* Boston, MA: South End Press, 1990.

Luker, Kristin. *Abortion & the Politics of Motherhood.* Berkeley and Los Angeles: University of California Press, 1984.

Melville, Keith, Ed. *The Battle Over Abortion.* Dayton, OH: National Issues Forums Institute, 1990.

Nathanson, Bernard N., M.D. *The Abortion Papers: Inside the Abortion Mentality.* New York: Frederick Fell Publishers, Inc., 1983.

Nathanson, Sue, Ph.D. *Soul Crisis: One Woman's Journey Through Abortion to Renewal.* New York: New American Library, 1989.

Simpson, Carolyn. *Coping With An Unplanned Pregnancy.* New York: The Rosen Publishing Group, 1990.

Szumski, Bonnie, Ed. *Abortion, Opposing Viewpoints.* St. Paul, MN: Greenhaven Press, 1986.

Terkel, Susan Neiberg. *Abortion: Facing the Issues.* New York: Franklin Watts, 1988.

Wennberg, Robert N. *Life in the Balance: Exploring the Abortion Controversy.* Grand Rapids, MI: William B. Eerdmans Publishing Company, 1985.

Magazines and Newspapers

"The Abortion Decision." *U.S. News and World Report*, August 7, 1989, 23-24.

Amidei, Nancy. "Variant Views on Abortion." *Commonweal*, October 26, 1990, 597-598.

Callahan, Daniel. "An Ethical Challenge to Prochoice Advocates." *Commonweal*, November 23, 1990, 681-687.

Carlson, Margaret. "Abortion's Hardest Cases." *Time,* July 9, 1990, 22-26.

Colen, B.D. "Mother, May I?" *Health*, October, 1990, 42-43.

Editor. "Abortion Polls." *Christianity Today,* December 17, 1990, 49.

Editor. "Too Many Abortions." *Commonweal*, August 11, 1989, 419-420.

Ehler, Bob. "Molly's Choice." *Star Tribune Magazine*, December 17, 1989, 5-13.

Fifteen American Women from Soujourner: The Women's Forum. "The Seamless Web Philosophy." *Utne Reader,* March/April, 1991. 61-63.

Frame, Randy. "Abortion Around the World." *Christianity Today,* February 19, 1991, 30-34.

Gardner, Charles A. "Is an Embryo a Person?" *The Nation,* November 13, 1989, 557-559.

Human Rights Alliance of Minnesota, Inc. Advertising Supplement, Spring 1991.

Hutchison, Sue, and James N. Baker. "The Right-to-Life Shock Troops." *Newsweek,* May 1, 1989, 32.

Jacobson, Jodi. "The Global Politics of Abortion." *Utne Reader,* March/April, 1991, 55-59.

Kantrowitz, Barbara. "Defying Simple Slogans." *Newsweek,* May 1, 1989, 36.

Kantrowitz, Barbara, et al. "The Crack Children." *Newsweek,* February 12, 1990, 62-63.

Kantzer, Kenneth S. "If Both Sides Would Listen...." *Christianity Today,* July 14, 1989, 36-38.

Kelly, James R. "Beyond Slogans: An Abortion Ethic for Women and the Unborn." *The Christian Century,* 184-186.

Lacayo, Richard. "Whose Life Is It?" *Time,* May 1, 1989, 20-24.

McDaniel, Ann. "The Nature of Abortion." *Newsweek,* July 17, 1989, 14-16.

Petchesky, Rosalind. "Giving Women a Real Choice." *The Nation,* May 28, 1990, 732-735.

Planned Parenthood. Brochure, quoting several prominent pro-life leaders.

Post, Stephen G. "Fetal Tissue Transplant: The Right to Question Progress." *America,* January 12, 1991, 14-16.

Sagan, Carl, and Ann Druyan. "Is It Possible To Be Pro-Life and Pro-Choice?" *Parade Magazine,* April 22, 1990, 4-8.

Saletan, William. "If Fetuses Are People...." *The New Republic,* September 18 & 25, 1989, 18-20.

Salholz, Eloise, et al. "The Battle Over Abortion," *Newsweek,* May 1, 1989, 28-32.

Salholz, Eloise, et al. "Politics and the Pill." *Newsweek,* February 26, 1990, 42.

Salholz, Eloise, et al. "Voting in Curbs and Confusion." *Newsweek,* July 17, 1989, 16-20.

Stafford, Tim. "The Abortion Wars." *Christianity Today,* October 6, 1989, 16-20.

Szegedy-Maszak, Marianne. "Calm, Cool, and Beleaguered." *The New York Times Magazine,* August 6, 1989, 18-20+.

Will, George F. "Mothers Who Don't Know How." *Newsweek,* April 23, 1990, 80.

Index

abortion(s)
  availability of, 12, 67-68, 75,
    88-89
  back-alley, 13
  bitterness about, 7-8
  characteristics of those
    obtaining, 9-10, 15
  in China, 78
  coerced, 55
  in Eastern Europe, 77-78
  effects of, 13, 35-36
  federal funding for, 64, 67-68,
    72-73, 88
  in Japan, 78
  laws, 61-65, 74
  and medical technology, 20,
    33-34, 64-65
  in Mexico, 81-82
  morality of, 53-55
  as murder, 8, 20-21, 53, 55
  number performed, 9
  obtaining, 43
  and politics, 48
  for poor women, 43, 68
  prevention of, 99
  procedures for, 82, 85-86
  in public hospitals and clinics,
    67
  in cases of rape and incest, 16,
    68-69, 96
  reasons for, 10-11, 23, 54
  reform, 43, 45, 61-63
  repeat, 12
  reporting requirements, 68, 77
  in Romania, 77
  rules for clinics, 68, 72-73, 77
  safety of, 81-83
  in the former Soviet Union,
    77-78
  spontaneous, 59
  underground, 89
abortion clinics
  attempts to close, 46
  blocking access to, 41, 48
  violence against, 45

Abortion Control Act, 73
abstinence, 99
abused children, 12
adoption, 16, 91-94, 96
  alternatives to, 96
  of crack babies, 94
  of handicapped children, 93-94
  of minority children, 93-94
  trauma of, 96
AIDS
  babies born with, 50, 94
Alan Guttmacher Institute, 17,
  78
amniocentesis, 83

baby brokers, 92
"Baby Choice," 39
Bell, Becky, 69-70
Bell, Bill and Karen, 70
birth control, 8, 10, 12, 27, 33, 36,
  50, 56, 78, 87, 99
Bonati, Frank, 92
Bush, George, 59, 68, 73, 92

Callahan, Daniel, 51, 54, 56
Caplan, Arthur, 29-30
Ceauşescu, Nicolae, 77
child abuse, 30
conception, 21, 28, 33, 54
contraception. See birth control
Cox, Archibald, 63

dilation and curettage, 82
dilation and evacuation, 82
drug-addicted babies, 55
"due process," 63

Ezell, Lee, 96

family planning clinics, 87
feminists, 17, 37
fetal abnormality, 83, 85
fetal development, 21-26
fetal rights, 8, 21, 28, 30-31, 45
fetal tissue, 59

gag rule, 72-73, 88
Gardner, Charles A., 22
Goldberg, Whoopi, 12-13, 14

Harding, Esther, 35-36
Hyde, Henry, 69

Kelly, James R., 57

Lambs of Christ, 46, 48
legislative process, 60-61
Lejeune, Jerome, 21
Luker, Kristin, 17, 34

McCorvey, Norma, 62
menstrual extraction, 89
"morning-after" pill, 85
motherhood, 17, 35-36

Najimy, Kathy, 53
Nathanson, Bernard, 18-19, 80
Nathanson, Sue, 13-14, 51
National Right to Life Committee,
    48, 69

O'Connor, Sandra Day, 65
Operation Rescue, 39-42, 45, 48,
    87

Paley, Grace, 37
parental consent laws, 64, 67,
    69-72, 74, 77
parenting skills, 98
personal privacy, right to, 62
physical intervention, 40
Planned Parenthood Federation of
    America, 68, 69, 87-88
Planned Parenthood v. Casey, 73,
    77
Post, Stephen G., 59
pregnancy, 10
    detection of, 30, 31, 33
    discrimination because of, 37
    risks of, 93
    teenage, 16, 72, 91-93, 96-99
privacy, right of, 63
pro-choice, defined, 7
pro-life, defined, 7

quickening, 33

Rabuzzi, Kathryn Allen, 36
Reagan, Ronald, 59, 64, 67

"rescues," 39
Right to Life Committee, 69
Roe v. Wade, 9, 61-65, 67, 73, 89
RU-486, 86

Sanger, Margaret, 87
Scheidler, Joseph, 53
sex education, 8, 50, 56, 99
sidewalk counselors, 39-40, 44, 48
Silent Scream, The, 19-20
social support systems, 56-58
Supreme Court, 9, 16, 21, 61, 63,
    67

Terry, Randall, 39-40, 42, 45, 50,
    87

"undue burden," 73, 77
unwanted children, 17, 55, 98

vacuum aspiration, 13, 82, 89
viability, 25-28, 63, 65, 67, 85

Wade, Henry, 62
Webster v. Reproductive Health
    Services, 21, 28, 67-68, 89
Weslin, Norman, 46
Wilke, John, 69
women's movement, 16, 43, 45
women's rights, 8, 45

Acknowledgments

American Portrait Films, Inc., pp. 18, 24, 80, 84 (both); Bill and Karen Bell, p. 70 (both); Collection of the Supreme Court of the United States, p. 62; Collection of the Supreme Court of the United States/National Geographic Society, p. 76 (top); Kerstin Coyle, p. 32 (bottom); Michael Evans, The White House, p. 64; Hayes Publishing Company, pp. 22, 23, 27; Jeffrey High/Image Productions, pp. 35, 56, 94, 95 (bottom); Hollywood Book and Poster, p. 14; Richard B. Levine, pp. 6, 30, 32 (top), 34, 49; Michigan Religious Coalition for Abortion Rights, p. 52 (bottom); National Organization for Women, p. 38 (top); Pro-life Action Ministries, pp. 24, 25, 26, 38 (bottom), 40, 43, 44 (bottom), 47 (bottom), 52 (top), 66, 90 (both); Jeff Tuttle/The Wichita Eagle, p. 42; Reuters/Bettmann, pp. 29, 76 (bottom), 79 (bottom); Francis M. Roberts, p. 95 (top); Jerome Rogers, p. 31; UPI Bettmann Newsphotos, pp. 41, 44 (top), 79 (top), 88, 93, 97.